I0536380

GRACE'S GIFT

Oregon Sky Book Six

KAY P. DAWSON

Grace's Gift: Oregon Sky Book Six
Print version
© Copyright 2022 (As Revised) Kay P. Dawson

CKN Christian Publishing
An Imprint of Wolfpack Publishing
5130 S. Fort Apache Rd. 215-380
Las Vegas, NV 89148

cknchristianpublishing.com

This book is a work of fiction. Any references to historical events, real people or real places are used fictitiously. Other names, characters, places and events are products of the author's imagination, and any resemblance to actual events, places or persons, living or dead, is entirely coincidental.

All rights reserved. No part of this book may be reproduced by any means without the prior written consent of the publisher, other than brief quotes for reviews.

Print ISBN 978-1-63977-231-5

GRACE'S GIFT

CHAPTER 1

"I'm real sorry for putting the frog in Susan's bonnet, Miss Hamilton. I promise I won't never do something like that again."

Grace smiled at the young boy in front of her, standing with his head down and eyes locked on the floor in front of him. "You won't '*ever*' do something like that again, Oliver."

He looked up with wide eyes and nodded his head fiercely. "That's what I said, ma'am. I won't never do it." His eyes darted to the open doorway and the sound of the other children playing outside before they made their way home from school.

She decided not to make this the time to try teaching the proper use of *ever* or *never* in his sentence and let him go join his friends. Oliver was usually well-behaved, and she knew he was a nervous child, so she didn't want to make him suffer any longer. He'd had a rough year after both of his parents died, leaving him to live with his grandmother.

Grace had already spoken to him privately after lunch when the incident happened and he knew he'd done wrong.

"You go on home now, Oliver. And just be sure you remember what I told you. It isn't nice to do something that will scare someone else."

"I know, ma'am. I'm real sorry."

He pulled his hat onto his head and raced to the door, obviously not wanting to take any chances that she was going to change her mind and keep him after school.

She went and stood in the doorway, wrapping her arms around herself and enjoying the heat from the fall sun on her cheeks. The days were still warm, but she knew winter was coming soon, so these were the kind of days to cherish before the cold hit.

Her eyes scanned the town around her and her heart swelled with love. When she'd arrived in this little community of Bethany as a young girl, she never could have imagined how much it would become her home.

She waved at Susan O'Hara who was outside the mercantile she ran with her husband, James. They had become like family to Grace as had so many others in the area.

Of course, her sister Phoebe had married into the Wallace family, who she was sure made up half the population anyway. So, in a way, they were all family.

Wagons bounced past, kicking dust up behind them as they made their way out of town. Some of the children were lucky enough to get a ride back to their farms but she knew many would be walking all the way home. At least she didn't have to worry about them out there on their own when the weather was nice like she did in the colder months.

Grace had been teaching now for almost a full year at this little church which had been built after the community lost the original one to a fire. When the townspeople had rebuilt, they'd made sure it would be able to house a small schoolhouse during the week for the growing population of children in the area.

She still couldn't believe how fortunate she'd been to be chosen as the first teacher for these children and it was a job she enjoyed more than anything.

She'd never had the chance to attend a proper school growing up, so she was determined to make sure her students got the best opportunity possible. Thankfully, she'd had her mother teach her from a young age until she passed away when Grace was just a child. Then, her sister had taken on the role of making sure she had an education the best she could. When they'd arrived in Oregon, Phoebe's new mother-in-law, Anna Wallace, had stepped into the job of teacher so Grace wasn't left behind in her studies.

Grace was almost certain with so many people involved in teaching her, she'd likely had more of an education than many children at some of the best schools in the country.

She took a few moments to tidy up the classroom to be ready for the morning, then grabbed her shawl from the hook to start making her way home.

Smiling to herself, she thought about the little house she was heading to. It wasn't much and, in truth, didn't have much more than the basic necessities, but the community had provided it for her to save her from having to come all the way from the farm outside of town where she'd been living.

This was her own place.

She'd lived with Phoebe and her husband Colton for the first few years after they'd arrived in Bethany and she was thankful they'd provided her with a home.

But, now they had twin children and Phoebe was expecting another baby soon. Grace knew they needed more space, so when the school board members had approached her, offering her the chance to live in the little house just on the other side of town, she'd gladly accepted.

It saved her from having to ride into town or spend the night at her brother's if the weather was bad. He was the sheriff in town and was now married and expecting a child of his own too.

It seemed like everyone had found someone to spend their lives with and Grace didn't want to be any more of a burden to them while they started their families. She wanted her independence and this house gave her some.

She ignored the little tug in her chest as she thought about how many people she'd witnessed falling in love over the past few years. She hoped someday she might have her own chance but she wasn't sure if it would happen.

There weren't many single men in the area and the one who'd held her heart since she was a thirteen-year-old girl had left town years ago.

Everyone still teased her about her crush on Connor Wallace, Colton's youngest brother.

He'd been a few years older than her when they'd first arrived in Oregon, and she blushed as she remembered how relentlessly she'd followed him around. She knew it had likely embarrassed him and she wished she hadn't been quite so fervent in her pursuit.

The thing was though, in her mind at least, it had never been a little crush. Even now, her heart skipped a beat when she thought of him although the memory had started to fade over the years.

She'd been sure what she felt in her heart had been real, even to her young mind.

"Grace! I'm glad we bumped into you. Would you like to come have supper with us tonight at Larsen's Boardinghouse? I've told your brother that, in my condition, I'm too tired to cook a meal today."

Grace laughed as she reached out to hug her sister-in-law, Sylvia, while her brother, Luke, stood beside his wife and rolled his eyes dramatically.

"She's still got a few days to go before this baby comes so I have a feeling we're going to be eating a lot of meals out."

"Well, I've told you many times you both are always welcome to come to my place. I know you haven't been feeling good, Sylvia, so any time you need a break from cooking, just let me know."

Grace knew how ill the other woman had been with her pregnancy and while her brother tried to act like he was annoyed at having to eat out, she knew he'd been doing everything possible to make life easier for his wife. If they weren't going to the boardinghouse or the saloon for a meal, Grace knew Luke had been doing the cooking and everything else he could help with.

"I will, Grace. But I don't like bothering you. After spending all day teaching, the last thing you need to be doing is caring for a pregnant woman who can't seem to stand the sight of most food without feeling queasy."

Grace laughed as Sylvia made a face, trying to make light of how sick she'd been over the past few weeks. "I wonder if it's just my brother's cooking that has caused this particular ailment?"

Luke raised an eyebrow in her direction. "I'm beginning to regret inviting you to join us." Sylvia playfully reached over and slapped his chest.

"Don't listen to him, Grace. I would love your company."

Tilting her head slightly, Grace pretended to contemplate her decision. "As much as I'd love to annoy my brother and join you both, the truth is,

I'm quite tired and was thinking of just heading home to have a bowl of soup."

"Well, make sure you stay inside once you get home. You never know who might be coming into town after dark."

Grace rolled her eyes and sighed loud enough for her brother to hear her clearly. "Luke, you know as well as I do that Bethany is perfectly safe. Even when some of the men head to the saloon in the evening, most of the time, everyone is well behaved. It's not like we're living back in St. Louis. Besides, I'm too tired to be out wandering around anyway."

Every night, her brother warned her to stay inside even though there had never been any real trouble in Bethany other than a few fights between men who'd had too much to drink at the saloon. But since the day she'd moved into the little house in town, he'd never stopped worrying.

"I know it's usually safe but you never know who will be riding into town. We've been getting a lot more drifters and strangers stopping around here and the last thing I need is to be worrying about you out on your own."

As if to emphasize his point, the sound of a horse whinnying loudly from the road leading into town interrupted their conversation. Luke squinted to see who it was, then slowly started to shake his head.

Grace turned to see who it was who had her brother so focused. The sun was behind the rider and she struggled to see clearly. She was sure it would be someone from Bethany and not some dangerous stranger who would make her brother's point for him.

"Just as I said. You never know who will be riding into town." Luke laughed loudly and walked toward the rider who was making their way over to them.

"Who is it?" Sylvia lifted her hand to shield the sun from her eyes as they watched Luke step off the wooden sidewalk onto the street.

Grace continued to squint until the rider got close enough for her to make out who it was. Her heart lurched as soon as she saw the man who was grinning down at her brother.

She couldn't believe what she was seeing and her voice was barely more than a whisper as she replied to Sylvia.

"Connor Wallace."

The man she'd thought about every single day since he left.

CHAPTER 2

"So you've finally decided to make your way back to Bethany."

Connor reined his horse in beside Luke, staying in the saddle and grinning down at the man he'd spent time with in California for a while looking for gold. They'd become good friends but when Luke had decided to come back to Oregon, Connor had stayed on to learn the blacksmith trade with a man who was willing to train him.

He'd wanted to stay and find his own adventure, away from the shadow of his large family who had all settled in Oregon. He'd dreamed of striking it rich and finding the excitement he'd never have back in a little town like Bethany.

If only he'd decided to come back with Luke, how different things might have been for him.

"I figured you'd be missing me by now so didn't think it'd be fair to stay away any longer."

He laughed as Luke scoffed, reaching up to shake his hand.

"Well, I can't say I've missed you but I imagine your mother will be excited to see you. Did you send a message to let anyone know you were coming home?"

"No, I thought I'd surprise them."

His eyes moved behind Luke to the two women watching them. One had dark hair and he was sure he'd never met her before. But the blonde woman beside her was the one who drew his attention. He knew instantly it was Grace and she was no longer the spindly little girl he remembered following him around everywhere.

"Grace."

He immediately felt like a complete fool. After riding up in front of a beautiful woman he'd known for years, all he could manage to say was her name like she was nothing more than a passerby.

"Connor, it's so good to see you again."

He could feel the genuine happiness in her voice. Grace had never been able to hide her emotions and everything came through when she spoke. He realized with a start how much he'd actually missed her.

But at the same time, he wished she wasn't standing here in front of him right now.

He'd known coming back to Bethany was going to be hard because he couldn't hide the scars he was carrying back with him. With the shadow of the sun behind him, he'd been careful to keep himself facing to the side when he rode up but he knew he couldn't hide forever.

He'd become accustomed to the stares and questions from strangers who met him but, now, being back with people who knew him, he wasn't ready to face their pity.

He knew that either Luke and his sister hadn't noticed anything different or they were just being polite by not asking about it.

The last thing he wanted to do was sit here and wait for them to ask.

"I'd better get out to the farm in time to be sure Ma has enough food to feed me supper. We'll catch up soon."

As he nodded in Grace's direction, he knew in that moment she'd seen what he'd been trying to hide. The sadness in her eyes left no doubt.

He quickly kicked in his heels and headed

through town, away from the questions he wasn't ready to answer.

❧❧❧

IT HADN'T TAKEN LONG for his brothers and his sister, Ella, to hear about his return. All of them were now sitting in his mother's house waiting for him to tell the stories from when he was gone and why he had finally decided to come home.

He knew they all had questions about the scar on the side of his face and the limp they would no doubt have noticed. But, he'd told his ma he was only going to explain it once so it would be better when everyone was here.

The mood had been excited and jovial ever since he'd arrived with everyone expressing how happy they were for him to be home. He'd had to meet all of the new members of the Wallace family who'd joined since he left, including his brother Logan's wife, Hope and her brother Max. Then there were the newest nieces and nephews who'd been born in his absence.

His mother's house at one time had seemed so big but, now, barely fit everyone inside the walls.

His niece, Sophia, the daughter of his oldest brother, Reid, had only been a toddler when he left, so seeing her now as a little girl talking and running around was a bit of a shock. She'd been staring at him shyly but he knew she wouldn't remember him.

While everyone visited, she walked over and stood in front of him, not making any effort to pretend she couldn't see his scars. He cringed inwardly, knowing what was coming.

"Uncle Connor, how did you get the marks on your face?"

"Sophia, mind your manners." Reid reached out his hand to pull his daughter back over to him.

Everyone had grown quiet and Connor knew it was time to just tell them everything. Well, as much as he was prepared to share.

"It's all right, Reid. It's not like no one else has noticed. I just didn't want to go through telling the story more times than I had to so it's easier to do it with you all here." He shrugged and absently brought his fingers up to the skin that was puckered all the way back around his ear.

"As you all know, I'd taken on work learning the trade of being a blacksmith while I was down in California. The man who'd let me work for him, Jeb Wolfe, was a widow with no children of his own. He took me in and shared his knowledge with me."

He took a breath and looked down at his hands, having a hard time meeting the looks of his family as he spoke. Bringing up the man who'd given so much to him caused his chest to tighten in pain as he remembered.

"He was a good man and he would've done just about anything for me. I was lucky to have met him."

Everyone remained silent while he swallowed and took a second before continuing.

"One morning, I was just arriving for work knowing Jeb would have likely been there since dawn as he always was. As I came from my room where I was staying above the cafe just down the street, I noticed smoke coming from the direction of the blacksmith shop. I raced toward it but, by the time I got there, flames had already engulfed the building. Other townspeople were there racing around trying to figure out what to do, screaming that Jeb was still inside."

"Oh, Connor. I'm sorry...." His sister reached over and put her hand on his leg.

But he was already back to that day in his mind as he had been so many times since then. It was hard to come back once he was there.

"I ran in, not even sure if I could get through the fire, but I had to try. I made it inside and I could see him caught under a large timber that had broken from the ceiling and there were already flames all around him. I heard him yelling at me, telling me to get out, but I couldn't leave him." He closed his eyes, wishing he could change what he was watching in his mind.

"I couldn't move it, no matter how hard I tried, and, the next thing I knew, another piece of the ceiling fell, pinning me on the ground by him. Pain shot through my leg and I knew something bad had happened. I must have passed out. The next thing I remember is Jeb pushing on the beam that had me pinned and yelling at me to get out. He was able to move it just enough for me to get my leg out but I couldn't stand. I tried pulling on the wood that had him trapped while he continued to holler for me to leave him. I just couldn't move it." His voice caught as he remembered the moment he'd looked at Jeb, meeting his eyes and knowing there was nothing he could do to help him.

"Before I could argue anymore, another man from town had managed to get inside and after seeing what was happening, he dragged me out about five seconds before the building collapsed."

Connor continued staring at the floor in front of him, needing a minute to bring himself back from that day. Everyone sat in silence around him, even the children who seemed to sense the enormity of the story they'd just heard even if they couldn't understand it all.

"Jeb didn't make it out and I was left with a long recovery to get over the burned skin and broken bones. Some days, I almost wish I hadn't been dragged out of that fire because I lost so much that day. Now, I live with a constant reminder every time I look in the mirror and see this face looking back at me."

"Connor Wallace, don't you *ever* say those words again. I'm sorry that you had to witness what happened to Jeb and it breaks my heart that you never let us know what had happened. Someone would have been down there to help you through it. But don't you ever think for a single moment that a scar changes the person inside. And there's not a person in this world who would think otherwise."

He knew his mother was wrong about that but he didn't think he needed to argue with her about it at the moment. It was enough that he'd shared the story of how he'd got the scars.

Finally, he lifted his gaze to look at the family

around him. Instead of the pity he was sure he would see, he could feel the outpouring of love from the faces staring back at him.

Sophia climbed up on his lap and touched his skin, the first person other than himself to run their fingers over the broken surface. He waited for her to pull her hand back in disgust but, instead, she smiled up at him.

"Miss Hamilton says everyone is made different and sometimes what makes a person different is what makes them special. I think you're handsome. It makes you look like a pirate."

The innocent words, spoken from a child who should be frightened by his looks, soothed the pain in his heart.

He decided he really should thank Miss Hamilton the next time he saw her.

CHAPTER 3

"It must have been so hard for him to be alone when all of that happened. Why didn't he come home sooner?"

Grace's eyes followed Connor as he pretended to race with the younger kids, falling down before the finish line while the children all climbed on top of him. Their laughter filled the air around them all as the family and friends from church gathered for one last outdoor picnic at Colton and Phoebe's before the colder weather settled in for the winter.

Phoebe had just filled her in on the story of what had happened to Connor while he was away and Grace's heart was filled with pain knowing what he'd gone through.

"I suspect there is more he isn't telling us but that's something he will need to do on his own time. So, whatever his reasons were for staying there, hopefully he can put it all behind him now that he's back home."

Grace could feel her sister's eyes on her. Phoebe knew how Grace had always felt about Connor. Everyone knew.

"He's still the same man though. He might have a few scars and a limp that will likely affect him for the rest of his life but other than a bit of lingering sadness from the events that led him back here, he's still Connor."

Grace turned to face Phoebe, pulling her eyebrows together in confusion. "Of course he is. Surely you don't think I would look at him any different."

Phoebe just shrugged then shook her head. "No, I didn't think you would. You're not that kind of person." Her sister moved her eyes to watch Connor. "But, I also know not everyone will be able to see past his scars. And I worry that he might have a hard time accepting how others will see him. It's going to take him some time to believe he's still the same man he was before. He was just a child himself when he left for California so it was a lot for him to handle on his own."

They watched him playing with the children who all seemed unconcerned with any outward appearances. They were having too much fun with someone who was willing to play with them to see anything else.

But, Grace had seen the looks from the people around them when the family had come into church this morning. And while the townsfolk from around here all knew him, and were happy to see him back home, there was no denying the fact that there was more than one second glance in his direction when they thought he wasn't looking.

Everyone was curious about the story that would explain what had happened to him.

So Grace knew things were likely much harder for him any time he had to be around strangers who hadn't ever known him before. They would only ever see the outward look without knowing who he was on the inside.

Thankfully, the people of Bethany were welcoming him home and hopefully soon, he wouldn't need to worry so much what anyone was thinking anymore.

Suddenly, he turned as he lifted one of the

twins in the air to spin them around and his eyes crashed into hers. His lips were still parted, as he laughed with the child in his arms, before he closed them into what she could only describe as a sad smile that didn't quite reach his eyes. Heat filled her cheeks and she held her breath, wishing she could quickly avert her eyes without it being obvious she'd been staring at him.

But her eyes didn't want to co-operate and it seemed like it took forever before he finally turned back to the child.

Her heart pounded loud in her ears and she swallowed to try and get her breathing under control. There had been something in his look that told her without saying a word that he was even more broken than he'd ever admitted to his family.

And no matter how hard she tried to figure out what she'd seen reflected in his eyes, the only thing her heart would let her know was that she was not going to let him give up.

Even if he already had.

"YOU KNOW, Bethany could use a permanent blacksmith. I'm sure Percy wouldn't miss having to come here once a week all the way from Skinner's Mudhole to do the work for people around the area. He's been doing that for a few years now, ever since Pete Granger moved back east and left us without a blacksmith. He's been using the old shop so I'm sure there wouldn't be much you'd have to do to get it ready."

Connor reached down and absently rubbed the ache in his leg as he bounced in the wagon seat next to his brother Reid. When his brother had stopped in at their mother's on his way to town to pick up feed, Connor had agreed to come for the ride. He'd been home for just over a week now and other than going to church yesterday, he hadn't had a chance to get into town and see how much it had changed while he was gone.

His chest tightened as the familiar pang of dread hit him. People were going to stare, some with pity, some with outright distaste. He knew people were going to want to ask questions but most would be too polite to ever say anything out loud.

It was always the same everywhere he went now and it was something he hoped in time he could get used to. The doctor had told him the redness of the scars would fade in time so maybe, eventually, they wouldn't be so noticeable.

The pain in his leg, however, wasn't something he believed would ever go away. Some days, the limp was barely noticeable but, days like today, he knew it was one more thing people would be staring at him for.

He tried to pretend it didn't bother him but it did.

Yesterday, while they'd been having their after church get-together, he'd seen the way Grace had looked at him and it had shaken him to the core.

The girl he'd always known who'd had a crush on him when they were younger was now looking at him with pity.

And he realized that was the only look he could ever hope for from a woman.

"I don't know. I haven't lifted a hammer since the accident. I'm not even sure I could."

He kept his eyes on the horizon as the town of Bethany came into view in the distance, ignoring the look he knew his brother was giving him.

"So, what are you planning to do then? Will you be helping with the farm? You know that's not something you ever had an interest in, least not the way Colton, Logan and I always have. It was never your dream to work on the farm."

Connor just shrugged. "Well, I don't have a

whole lot of options open to me, so I guess that's likely what I'll do."

Reid sighed loudly, so he turned to face his older brother. Reid wasn't even trying to hide his annoyance. "Connor, you would be miserable working the farm and you know it. Bethany needs a blacksmith and that's something you took the time to learn how to do. So, why wouldn't you want to do that? It doesn't make any sense."

Connor didn't even know what to say in reply because it didn't make any sense to him either. He'd loved learning the blacksmith trade with Jeb and it was something he'd finally believed he was truly good at. He'd never had the same interest in farming that his brothers, and even his sister, had always had. Part of the reason he'd left for California was to find something else that could excite him.

And he'd found that when he'd taken that job with Jeb. But, after the accident, he just didn't know if he could ever go back to it. And he knew it wasn't just because of the physical problems he might have with the work.

The memories of that moment in the fire haunted him and guilt that he'd survived and not Jeb tore him apart. He knew every time he lifted the hammer to pound onto the iron, he would feel the guilt of being able to still do the job old Jeb had loved so much.

It didn't make sense to him so he didn't know how he could explain it to anyone else either.

But, part of him had died in that fire too, and he wasn't sure if he could ever get it back.

CHAPTER 4

"Just wait here with me, Sophia. Your father will be here soon. You and Max can play on the swings while you wait."

Grace turned and used her hands to sign to Max and tell him the same thing. The young boy had become a part of the Wallace family when his older sister married Logan so they'd all taken the time to learn how to communicate with the child who'd been born deaf. He was ten years older than Sophia but he took his older cousin job seriously so Grace knew he would keep an eye on the young girl until Reid showed up to take them back out to the farm.

She sat on the steps and watched the two remaining children play, the sound of Sophia's laughter filling the air around them. All of the other students had been picked up or started their walk home but Reid must have been running late. The family always had someone coming in or out of town so whoever was available made sure the Wallace children made it to and from school.

And soon, all the younger Wallace children would be coming too, filling the small school to the brim. It seemed like everyone around her was happily married and having babies every time she turned around.

Grace loved them all even though she wasn't a true member of the family. She was just the sister to Phoebe - someone who had married into the Wallace family but they all made sure she always knew she was welcome.

It didn't make it easier though, as she sometimes felt like she was standing to the side and watching everyone else living their new lives while she wasn't sure where she fit in anymore. She was truly happy for both her sister and her brother, Luke, but she still had the days where she wondered when it would be her turn.

Bethany was a small community, and everyone already knew everyone, so she was aware there weren't really any men around her age who lived here. She'd tried to convince herself she would be happy if she never did find that true love she'd dreamed of and she could continue teaching the children who needed her without needing to settle down and have children of her own.

But she knew, deep down, she longed for the same happiness she saw when her sister looked at Colton or when she held her babies in her arms.

The sound of a wagon coming around the corner reached her ears. She lifted her head and was hit with the familiar pounding in her chest when she saw Connor sitting beside Reid in the front. They stopped just up the wide street across from the school, in front of the old blacksmith shop.

Reid waved over at her, so she stood up and called to Sophia. The children came over to her, with the young girl skipping ahead, already about to cross the street.

"Daddy!"

Max took the girl's hand and they all walked across to where Connor and Reid were now standing beside the wagon. Reid crouched down and let Sophia race into his arms before standing up with her arms wrapped around him tightly.

"I thought you'd forgot us!"

Grace laughed and shook her head. "I tried to

tell her you hadn't forgot her. And even if you had, I would make sure they got home safe."

"Sorry we're late. It took us a bit longer to load up the feed at the mill than we'd planned. I knew you'd make sure they were looked after until we got here."

Grace nodded then looked over at Connor who was leaning against the wagon. He quickly averted his eyes when she caught him staring and her heart fluttered slightly. "It's nice to see you, Connor."

They'd spoken a few times since he'd been back but it always felt awkward. She knew he likely always thought about the times she'd chased after him like a love-sick puppy and he wanted to keep her at a distance in case she got any thoughts of continuing the behavior now that he was back.

He'd always made it clear back then he was never interested in her and had been sure to let her know his feelings in that area hadn't changed since he was home. So she wasn't about to embarrass herself over a man who obviously would never return her feelings.

But, since they were going to always be around each other in the small community and at family gatherings, the least he could do is try to be civil.

"You too, Grace. Sorry we're late. Reid is determined to drag me to look at this dilapidated building that used to be a blacksmith shop, even though I've assured him I'd be just as happy back working on the farm."

Grace pulled her eyebrows together. "You? You never enjoyed working on the farm. Wasn't that why you wanted to go to California in the first place?"

Connor sighed loudly and rolled his eyes as Reid laughed and nodded his head emphatically. "That's exactly what I said, Grace. He has never wanted to be a farmer. Bethany needs a blacksmith so it's the perfect answer for everyone."

Grace walked around the wagon to step onto the wooden landing in front of the old shop. "Oh, this will be perfect for you Connor! And it would save Percy from having to come here all the time."

The rest of them walked around and stood in front of the building. Connor lifted his hand to shield his eyes from the sun as he looked up. "I don't know. It looks like it's about to fall to the ground. Who even owns the building? Even if I did want to get back to working as a blacksmith, it's not like I have a fortune to invest in buying the building and putting it back together."

"When the old blacksmith moved back east, he just sold it James O'Hara for a low price to be rid of it. James had thought he could use it for storage but it's been left with all of the equipment and everything needed for Percy to use when he came. I'm sure James would be more than happy to let you use it even if you don't want to buy it from him. Just having a blacksmith in town again would be a huge benefit to everyone in the area." Reid carried Sophia over to the door where the lock hung open. "James said he'd open it so you could take a look around."

Grace watched as Connor glared at his older brother. "So, you'd already spoken to James before even talking to me about it?"

But Reid just shrugged and ignored him as he opened the door and walked inside. Grace held her smile back as she knew all of the Wallace men were terribly stubborn so Connor wouldn't be able to make Reid feel guilty.

It also meant that Connor was just as likely to argue against it.

She walked in behind Reid and looked around. It was a bit run-down but she really didn't expect a blacksmith shop to be as neat and tidy as a schoolhouse would be. "It just needs a bit of a sort out...and maybe a dusting. It wouldn't be hard to get it looking good again." She looked around, running her finger over the wooden workbench where tools were strewn all over the place. She didn't want to let on how much she was worried it would be too big of a job for anyone to take on. "I'd say Percy wasn't too worried about keeping things clean since it's not really his place. He was just filling in until someone permanent could take over."

Connor was standing just inside the doorway, slowly looking around at the mess in front of them. She watched as he closed his eyes and breathed deeply. There was something in his eyes when he opened them again that gave her hope.

"This could be all yours, Connor. Just think what all you could do. I know the man who spent so many hours teaching you would be so proud to see you doing something you enjoyed. He wouldn't want you just throwing all of that time learning the trade away when you have the perfect opportunity right here in front of you."

She held her breath, hoping she hadn't pushed him too hard with her words. But she had to say it, hoping to get him to see what she could tell was in his heart.

Max wandered around, picking up random tools and setting them down before moving to the next one. Connor kept his eyes on the boy but Grace could see his jaw moving as he played her words over in his mind.

"Jeb always planned for me to take over for him."

"Well, sometimes life has other plans. And while you won't be taking over for him, you'll be keeping his memory alive by continuing to do what he taught you. That's something I'm sure he would have wanted."

Reid walked over and cupped his hand on Connor's shoulder as he continued. "Besides, I seem to remember the last time you helped me on the farm I found you face down, dragging behind the plow as the horse made his way back to the barn."

Connor's mouth opened in shock that his brother would bring up such a sensitive memory and a crease formed between his eyes. "I was only twelve years old when that happened! I shouldn't have even been left to do that work on my own when there's no way I had the strength to handle the job."

Reid just laughed. "Well, you wouldn't stop demanding to have more responsibility. So I had to show you somehow. But, I think we all knew then there was no way you were ever going to be working on the farm. You've found what you're meant to be doing and it'd be a shame to let it pass you by."

Grace watched the exchange, hoping Reid was getting through to Connor. He reached out and lifted one of the tools that Max had inspected and set back down on the workbench. When he lifted his head, their eyes met.

"I think it's meant to be, Connor. Bethany needs a blacksmith."

"What if my heart isn't in it anymore? What if I physically can't do the work anymore?"

For a moment, Grace could see the young man she remembered before he left all those years ago. Except, back then, he was so full of hope and excitement for the adventures to be had in life.

Now, he was scared to let himself hope for anything more than what he believed was available to him.

"You're not going to know unless you try. I've known you for a long time and you've never backed down from a challenge. If you end up hating what you're doing, it doesn't mean you're stuck doing it forever." She smiled widely as she spoke to him, hoping he would listen. "And as far as not being able to physically do the work, I don't believe that. I sat and watched you throw the children around without any trouble when you were all playing the other day. I couldn't tell who was having more fun, by the way."

He was looking at her so intently and, for a moment, she forgot that Reid and the children were still in the room. Finally, the corners of his mouth lifted and he pushed his hand through his hair.

"Well, since the two of you have already decided this is what I'm going to be doing, I guess it'd be rude of me to not at least give it a try." He reached down and ran his finger through the thick layer of grime on the work surface. "But, since you're both so determined I do this, I expect a whole lot of help cleaning this place up."

Reid glanced at her and grinned. She could tell how happy Connor's brother was that he'd managed to convince him to go back to doing what he truly loved.

Grace laughed and nodded. "Lucky for you, there's nothing more I love than the challenge of making something a little run-down even better than ever."

CHAPTER 5

"You know, I wasn't really serious when I said I wanted help cleaning. Truth is, I could likely do things a whole lot quicker on my own." Connor placed a hammer next to the iron, then reached up and wiped at his brow.

He looked around at the people who'd showed up to help, unable to hide his smile knowing how hard they were all trying to get this building cleaned up for him. He'd lost count of how many times he reminded them about the fact it was a blacksmith shop and it really wasn't meant to be spotless.

After his first day of work, things were going to be a dirty mess anyway.

But, they'd insisted on helping him to sort and see what he had to use for tools before he started work. Colton was in the far corner looking through a trunk, throwing things onto the floor as he speculated about what the tool would be used for. Logan was signing something to Max who had shown a lot of interest in everything inside the building and how it worked. His sister's husband, Titus, was helping Luke lift a large anvil to the side so they could pull even more scattered tools out from behind it. Reid had gone to the lumber yard to get some wood to do some repairs to the floor.

The lone woman who'd said she would help was furiously scrubbing his work bench, her sleeves rolled up past her elbows as she scrunched her face up in concentration. She'd wrapped a kerchief over her hair to keep it from falling in her face as she worked but a few pieces had already worked their way free, now framing her dirt-smudged face.

He didn't have the heart to tell her that the grease and oil stains in the wood would never come out, no matter how hard she scrubbed. And even if they somehow did, those pieces of wood were going to be just as dirty a week from now.

She'd been determined to help however she could, so had shown up with a bucket in hand ready to clean first thing this morning. And she'd been working non-stop ever since without a single complaint.

"You're likely right about that. But you know how Ma is and if we weren't here doing our share to help you out, we'd never hear the end of it. So, you're stuck with us, whether you like it or not." Colton lifted a piece of metal out of the box he was sorting, shaking his head as he set it on the ground beside him. "But to be completely honest, I think it might have been easier for you to just throw everything out of here and start over with new tools. Half this stuff is junk."

Connor chuckled and walked over to his brother and picked up the piece of metal he'd discarded. "See, what you see as junk, I can picture as a possible rim for a wagon. Or, maybe a box of nails to build a new home."

"Or a new set of shoes for your brother-in-law's prized stallion." Titus came over and slapped him on the shoulder with a wide grin.

"Yes, I've already promised you that the shoes for your stallion will be the first job I finish."

"What about my new pitchfork? I've only got two tines left and it doesn't make for an easy job cleaning out the stalls." Logan called over to them, making sure Connor didn't forget his order when he got the shop opened.

He laughed at his brothers and shook his head before heading back to sorting the tools he'd been looking through. The man who'd been here previously had left everything behind and as Percy had come in to fill the needs of the town, it seemed like the building had become a place to just dump everything without any care. Since it wasn't his business, he didn't have the same pride he likely did for his own shop in Skinner's Mudhole.

But Connor was already starting to feel some pride for the small building that was his now, imagining what it could become. He ignored the niggling worry of what could also happen, like it had in Jeb's shop.

He swallowed hard and pushed the thoughts away, turning quickly and stepping on something soft under his foot.

"Ouch!"

His hands reached out to steady the small body he'd ran into, quickly grabbing her shoulders as she hopped onto one foot, glaring up at him. He fought the sudden laughter that threatened to spill out at the look she was giving him. It was so out of place with the dirt-smudged nose and fiery red cheeks.

He didn't think a woman could be so beautiful when looking like she had been rolling around in a dirt pile. Yet here was Grace, the girl who'd grown into a woman he never could have imagined from that girl who used to follow him everywhere.

"I'm sorry. I didn't know you were there."

She rolled her eyes and turned her head slightly, muttering under her breath. He couldn't be sure but he was almost certain she'd said something to the effect of him never knowing she was there.

She pulled back and he let his hands drop to his sides. "I've been standing in this same spot for almost an hour, scrubbing these old, stained pieces of wood. I guess you didn't notice me."

"I noticed you, Grace. And I do appreciate everything you've done to help me today. I guess I was just lost in my thoughts and didn't realize I'd stepped over so close to you."

She shrugged nonchalantly before reaching back into her bucket of soapy water. "Well, I'm not sure if I'll ever get this work bench completely clean. I don't know what else I can try."

Connor smiled at her as she started scrubbing again, lifting a soap-covered hand up to push a stray strand of hair out of her eyes. It left a large white mound of bubbles on her forehead and he couldn't stop himself from reaching out to wipe it off before the soap slid down into her eyes.

Her head snapped up as soon as his thumb touched her skin, her eyes holding his. He'd forgotten just how blue her eyes were.

He quickly brought his hand back, showing her the suds on the tip of his finger. When she saw what he'd actually been doing, her cheeks flushed an even darker shade of red and her own hand went back up to her face, desperately wiping at any more soap that might be left.

He knew he'd rattled her by touching her like that but he hadn't been able to help himself.

She turned away, pushing the cloth back and forth over the wooden surface she'd almost scrubbed raw. The redness of her cheeks had spread to her ears and his chest tightened with guilt for embarrassing her.

But, if he was being completely truthful, he knew Grace wasn't the only one who'd been rattled by a simple touch. And he needed to make sure it never happened again because even if Grace did believe she had feelings for him after all this time, he wasn't going to let her mistake her pity for anything more.

CHAPTER 6

"Miss Hamilton, the boys won't let me play marbles with them. Oliver says I'm too little and don't know what I'm doing."

Oliver's sister Lizzie pulled on her skirt as she looked up at Grace with her big brown eyes filled with tears. The cool breeze had given the young girl's cheeks a rosy blush and her long hair blew beneath the bonnet tied tightly on her head.

Grace crouched down so she could be on eye level with Lizzie, taking her hands in hers. "Well, Lizzie, sometimes the older boys like playing games among themselves. Maybe you could play something with the other girls instead and I will talk to Oliver about letting you play some time when he can teach you how to play."

"But I want to play marbles now. The girls are playing hide and seek, but I don't want to play that."

Grace looked over at the small group of boys playing marbles next to the front steps of the school. Poor Oliver always had his sister tagging along after him and he tried to be patient but some days he just wanted to play with his own friends. He was part of the small group of boys who were quiet and usually didn't cause too much trouble, other than the odd frog in a girl's bonnet.

There were some older boys who sometimes liked to give the others trouble but they were playing a game of catch and not bothering with the others, so Grace hated to ruin their fun by insisting they let the little girl play with them.

"Why don't you walk with me a bit and we'll see if we can find the girls hiding?" Grace wanted the girl to start making friends with some of the other girls so she wasn't so dependent on her brother.

Since their parents had died, she'd become like a shadow to Oliver.

Lizzie glanced over at her brother with her bottom lip trembling. Grace caught Oliver's eye and she could tell he was feeling bad for not letting his sister play. So, she winked and let him know she would look after Lizzie for him.

She stood up, taking Lizzie's hand and started to walk over to Sophia who was resting her head against a tree and counting loudly.

"Nineteen...twenty! Ready or not, here I come!"

Sophia turned quickly, almost running into them as she started hunting for her friends.

"Sophia, would you mind if Lizzie and I help you look for the girls?"

She knew Sophia wasn't the type to ever exclude anyone even if the other girl was a couple of years younger than her. It didn't matter to her because she wanted to be friends with everyone.

"Okay, but you have to make sure you touch them if you see them before they run back to home which is this tree."

Grace smiled to herself as Sophia tried to explain to Lizzie what the rules were. But, the younger girl still held tightly to Grace's hand so she was going to have to help her look.

They raced around the schoolyard, looking behind every tree and any other spot the girls could be hiding. Lizzie was laughing loudly as some girls raced past them for home and she squealed with excitement when she tagged one of them out.

All of the girls were having fun, especially now that their teacher was playing with them too. And, Grace had to admit, she was enjoying herself playing a game she hadn't played in a few years. Just because she was a grown woman now, it didn't mean she couldn't enjoy a good game of hide and seek, now and then.

"Now it's your turn to count Miss Hamilton!"

The girls were so excited she was certain she'd never be able to get them to do any schoolwork after they got back in from lunch. But, the weather was so nice outside today and she knew there wouldn't be many more days like this, so she was going to let the children enjoy it.

She leaned her forehead against the tree and squeezed her eyes shut as she started counting out loud. The poor girls were giggling so loud it wasn't going to be hard to find any of them but she would be sure to make it at least seem like she was struggling.

"Give me back my marble! That's my favorite one."

Loud shouting and yelling interrupted her counting, so Grace quickly pulled back and looked toward the boys who'd been playing marbles. The older boys had stopped their game of catch and were now over there and the largest boy, Dirk, was holding something above his head out of the reach of Oliver.

"Well, it's mine now."

Grace hitched up her skirt and raced over before things got out of control but she could already see she wasn't going to make it in time. All of the younger boys were yelling and the older boys were laughing as they tried to impress Dirk by acting like him.

"Boys! Stop this instant." She ran over and reached for Dirk's arm just as he drew it back to throw the marble into the bush behind the school. As he threw it, his arm caught her shoulder, sending her to the ground. She landed flat on her face in the dirt by their feet.

"Miss Hamilton, are you all right?"

Sophia's voice cut through the sudden silence as all of the children moved back, now realizing they were likely in a lot of trouble.

She got to her knees, trying to wipe at her eyes with one hand while she worked to get her emotions under control. The last thing she wanted to do was to say something to the boys out of anger. Not to mention the embarrassment she was fighting over being flung to the ground in front of all of her students.

"Get out of the way. What is going on here? Grace, are you okay?"

Connor's voice reached her ears and she squeezed her eyes shut tight, trying to pretend she hadn't heard him. Of course, she should have known he would witness her humiliation.

He crouched down beside her to take her hand, resting one hand on her shoulder. She slowly opened her eyes and offered him a smile. "Oh, yes, I'm quite good. Nothing like eating some dirt for lunch."

As she said the words, she had to reach up and wipe some mud that was stuck to her lip.

"Well, you shouldn't have tried getting in the middle of anything." He pulled her to standing beside him, continuing to hold her steady as she brushed the dirt from her skirt.

"I'm fine, Connor. And I'm the teacher. I have to get in the middle of things."

She pulled away from him, aware that all of the children were still standing around, scared to even move. They'd never witnessed their teacher being thrown to the ground before so they were all terrified of what was about to happen.

Connor turned to Dirk and walked over to

stand in front of him. "Young man, you better apologize to Miss Hamilton."

Dirk looked around at his friends who were watching intently then shrugged, stuffing his hands into his pockets. "Sorry, ma'am. I didn't know you were coming behind me. I didn't knock you down on purpose."

Grace took a deep breath and glanced around at the students. "Girls, you can all go back inside and take your seats. I'm going to talk with the boys and we'll be in shortly." She crossed her arms in front of her chest and turned back to face Oliver as the girls ran up the steps and closed the door behind them.

"Oliver, do you want to tell me what happened?"

His eyes were wet with tears he was desperately fighting to hold back as he looked at her. "We were just playing marbles when they came over and kicked them. Then Dirk took my favorite one and threw it in the bush. That's when you came over."

"Dirk, is that true?"

The older boy just shrugged again, smirking over at his friends without saying anything.

"Young man, your teacher has asked you a

question." Connor was still standing to the side with his own arms crossed in front of him.

Dirk rolled his eyes before speaking. "They're just a bunch of dumb marbles. I didn't mean to kick them. I was walking past and accidentally stepped on them."

"And what about the one you picked up and threw in the bush? Was that an accident too?" Grace was trying hard to be patient but Dirk was proving to be even more of a handful today than he usually was. She didn't want to admit it but, sometimes, she was afraid of the boy's temper she'd witnessed sometimes. He was at least a head taller than her and was a heavy-set young man who was intimidating to all of the other children. Knowing Connor was still standing there helped make her feel a bit safer as she tried to find out what happened.

Dirk looked at Oliver and laughed. "He's a big baby. It's just a marble."

Connor moved closer to the boy and Grace had to quickly put her hand on his arm to stop him. "Dirk, I've had enough from you today. I want you to head home and I will come out after school to speak with your parents."

He laughed again as he turned to walk away.

"Go ahead. My pa isn't going to be happy that you sent me home."

Grace's stomach clenched in dread because she knew he was right. Mr. Matthews was known to be a hard-headed man around town who liked to bully anyone he didn't think was treating him fairly. She knew it wasn't going to be easy to go out and talk to him but she had to try.

Dirk had become too disruptive to the other students and they all shouldn't have to be scared in their own classroom.

"Boys, you can all go in and I will talk with the rest of you in a bit." She could see Oliver was torn as his tear-stained eyes looked toward the bush, not wanting to leave his marble behind. But she also knew all of the children were going to be worked up so she couldn't let them all be inside on their own.

"Miss Hamilton, would it be all right if I take Oliver and see if we can find that marble? You can go on inside and get the other students settled. I'm sure it won't take us long."

She smiled gratefully at Connor, thankful he'd recognized the need and stepped in to offer to help the boy. She nodded and watched him put his hand on Oliver's shoulder, talking to him as they walked toward the bush. He was making sure

Oliver didn't feel bad for crying over a marble and she sent up a little prayer that they'd somehow find the small piece of glass in the trees.

It might be just a marble but she sensed that Connor wasn't prepared to stop until he'd found it for the boy.

CHAPTER 7

"You didn't need to drive me out here. I'm perfectly capable of managing with Luke's wagon on my own."

Grace grabbed onto the seat as they hit a bump, and she quickly glanced over at Connor. "In fact, I'd say I might even be a better driver. I would at least try to miss the bad spots on the road."

He grinned, keeping his eyes on the road ahead. She wished she could reach out and wipe away the scar that covered this side of his face and take away the memories of how he got it. At least he didn't spend as much time trying to hide it from her as he had when he first came home.

Now, he mostly did that with strangers. She

hoped it meant he was starting to accept that everyone who cared about him could see beyond the redness of his skin.

"I have no doubt you could drive this wagon just fine but Luke made it clear he didn't want you coming out here by yourself. He can't take you, so you're stuck with me. From what your brother says, Darius Matthews isn't the kind of man you want to be confronting on your own."

Luke had been adamant she wasn't going out to speak with Dirk's father but Grace knew, if she didn't, Dirk would think he'd got away with his behavior.

So, Connor had agreed to go with her. He'd closed his shop early and they were on their way to the Matthews' farm before dark settled in. The days were shorter now with the approach of winter so she was actually relieved she wouldn't have to worry about being out by herself if it took longer than expected.

She wasn't afraid of meeting with Mr. Matthews on her own but she hated the thought of ever having to be out in the middle of nowhere in the dark by herself.

"Thanks for helping Oliver find his marble. I honestly thought it would be lost forever among all those trees and brush. I know it took you longer than you likely expected."

Oliver had come back into the classroom about an hour after the lunch break, happily holding his marble. Grace had felt bad knowing Connor had spent that long crawling around in the bushes with the boy.

"Honestly, I didn't think we were going to find it either but I had to try. The poor boy was obviously upset." He looked over at her with a serious expression. "It was a gift from his father. It was the last one he remembered getting from his pa before he died so he told me it was special. And he said he wasn't going to bring it to school anymore because he never wanted to lose it again."

"Oh, that poor child. I know how hard it's been since his parents died." She shook her head sadly. "Poor Oliver."

She was so glad he'd been able to open up to Connor about the marble. To everyone else, it was silly for him to be so upset over it but now she completely understood what he was feeling.

She'd been the same way over things she'd got from her own parents before they'd died. Absently, she looked down and ran her fingers over the shawl that was showing signs of wear.

She wore it often, even over top of her coat sometimes, because it was something she remembered her ma wearing. Her memories of her parents were fading because she had been so young when they died. So, she held on to everything she could that kept them alive in her mind.

Connor turned back to the road, working the reins to lead the horses away from a large rock lying in the middle of the track. She quickly grabbed for the seat again so she wouldn't tumble out of the wagon onto the ground.

He glanced at her with a sheepish grin. "Sorry."

She continued holding the seat but smiled back at him. "I've already had a mouthful of dirt today, so try not to dump me onto the ground."

"I'm not used to driving a wagon. I've got used to just riding my horse everywhere I need to go. I don't think I've been behind the reins since I left for California."

"Well, I would have been perfectly fine with just riding my horse too, but I know how much everyone thinks that's not proper for me to do. It seems like what was fine a couple years ago when I was still a child in everyone's mind is no longer acceptable. Plus, being the school teacher, I guess I need to set a good example."

Grace had taken to riding as soon as they'd arrived in Bethany and it was something she loved. Even if everyone said she should be riding sidesaddle, it wasn't something she'd ever been able to do. She wondered if Connor would be shocked to know she rode astride.

"Your sister, Ella, took me under her wing when I was younger and taught me to ride a horse on a regular saddle. She even showed me how to sew up some of my old skirts so that they were like pants when I wanted to ride." She watched to see his reaction. Most people around Bethany were used to Ella, and her, riding around on their horses like men.

He laughed and shook his head. "I remember watching you learn to ride the first time. And over the next few months, it seemed like you were always around so I suspected you were going to end up loving it as much as Ella."

"You watched me learning to ride?"

She was mortified to think that the young teenage Connor she'd had such a crush on had watched her falling repeatedly as she tried to learn to ride like Ella.

He shrugged nonchalantly, carefully steering the horses to avoid a dip in the road. "I'd just come back from town with feed and headed into the barn. You and Ella were over in the corral with your sister and Colton." He glanced over and laughed. "I guess that was likely when you learned how to go face down in the dirt and keep getting up."

Her cheeks burned as she was reminded about today.

"How did you even see what was going on over at the school grounds today anyway? Were you spying on me?"

Connor had been in his shop now for over a week and, while he'd sometimes been coming or going when they were outside at recess, she hadn't really seen much of him otherwise. He seemed busy already with work and was usually still working past the time she walked home for the day.

He'd moved into a room at Larsen's Boarding-house, for the time being, which was close to her little house. She could see it from her front window and she'd found herself watching from time to time to see if she would spot him.

"I wouldn't call it spying exactly. I'd gone outside for some fresh air and sunshine when I spotted you running around playing a game with the children. I might have secretly been wishing I could go over and play too."

She rolled her eyes and laughed, shaking her head in embarrassment. "It was an exciting game of hide and seek. I'm sure the children would have loved having another adult join in the fun."

"I saw what was happening with the boys and was already heading over when you raced into the middle of it all."

Just then, they came around the bend that led to the Matthews' house and her heart started to race. She wasn't the kind of person who could handle confrontation well so she was worried about what she would say.

As she gripped her hands tightly together, she quickly peeked over at Connor, grateful to have him with her. He gave her an encouraging smile as he pulled the wagon to a stop by the house. "Don't worry about Darius Matthews. I've known you long enough to know he doesn't stand a chance against you." He hopped down then came around the wagon to offer his hand up to her.

"And, if he does decide to give you any trouble, he'll have to answer to me."

Knowing Connor was with her and he believed she could handle this gave her the courage she needed to face Dirk's father.

She ignored the heat that raced through her

body as he took her hand and hoped he didn't notice how much it affected her.

Right now, she needed to forget the Grace who quite obviously still had the crush on the boy beside her and become the teacher who wasn't going to let a student disrespect her in her classroom.

CHAPTER 8

"Connor, you don't need to come over here every day and check on the wood stove. That's the job the bigger boys are supposed to be taking care of."

Connor pushed another log into the stove then closed the grate. He stood up and wiped his hands down the front of his pants. "Well, I'm right across the street and it makes me feel better knowing the school is warm enough for the children."

He knew his excuse sounded pathetic but he couldn't really come out and tell her he thought it was a good idea for him to be here during the lunch break each day until they knew Dirk wasn't going to act up any more.

Ever since the day a week ago when he'd gone

with Grace to speak to Darius Matthews, Connor worried about what Dirk could do. His father had been rude and condescending to Grace and it had been all Connor could do not to punch the other man in the nose for the way he spoke to her. She'd handled it well and hadn't backed down, insisting that Dirk be punished for his behavior at school that day. Now, Connor figured Dirk might be angry enough with his teacher to cause more problems.

He was a large enough boy to make Connor wary of her being on her own with him. But there was no way he'd ever let her know that. He knew she would be angry with him for not believing she could handle things on her own.

The children were all putting their heavy coats and hats on to go outside and play after eating their lunch inside. It was bitterly cold today and he was sure he could smell snow in the air.

"I appreciate your help but you really don't need to worry. We managed to get through the winter last year without anyone coming and putting wood in the fire before the school day started or keeping it stoked up during the day."

She was crouched down helping Lizzie tie her hat tightly under her chin. "Now Lizzie, you stay with Sophia and if anyone needs anything, come in and get me. I'm going to grade some papers and will join you soon."

The young girl nodded, then walked out the door with Sophia and some of the other children. Grace stood back up and smiled at him, crossing her arms in front of herself. "Besides, if Dirk decides to cause any trouble, I can always send one of the other boys over to get you, if that would make you feel better."

His cheeks burned as he walked over and sat down on one of the pews that were used as desks during the week. He pulled a sandwich out of his pocket and took a big bite, hoping it would give him a few seconds to come up with an excuse.

"That's not why I'm coming over here. Did you ever think maybe I just like having some company to eat my lunch with? And it's nicer here than sitting in my dirty workshop."

She laughed softly and walked past him to go sit at the front behind her own desk. "I'm sure it is nicer in here but I'm also sure Mrs. Larsen would be more than happy to make you lunch every day at the boardinghouse."

He raised an eyebrow in her direction. "So, you're telling me you'd rather get up extra early, come into a cold school every morning and then spend the day bringing wood in yourself from out back? When you have a perfectly capable man willing to do it for you?"

"No, I appreciate the fact that you're starting the fire in the morning. It is much nicer to come into a building that's already warmed up. But, I can manage to keep the fire going throughout the day with the help from the boys."

He knew she was right but he also knew he wasn't going to stop coming over until he knew for sure Dirk wasn't going to retaliate for her going out to speak to his father.

He watched her as she looked down at the papers in front of her. Her golden hair was tied up in a bun on top of her head today and, from the angle he was looking at her, he could see her long eyelashes move as she read over the page.

His pulse quickened and he quickly looked toward the window when she lifted her head. "But, since you mentioned him, has Dirk caused any trouble this week?"

"Not any more than usual. I'd say he's determined to prove himself again to the boys he's friends with and has been a bit ruder to me. But, I can handle him. His father said this is the last year he'll be in school anyway. I just need to keep things under control until he's not here influencing the other boys anymore."

Darius Matthews had informed them the family was moving back to Chicago where his family was from. He'd been sure to mention that one of the reasons they were moving was because they didn't believe Dirk could receive a proper education from a backwoods schoolhouse and a teacher who'd never even attended a real school on her own.

Connor didn't know if that really was one of the reasons or it was just the father's way of striking out at the teacher who was demanding his son be punished but he didn't care what the reasons were for them leaving Bethany. He didn't think there was anyone around here who would miss a man like him anyway.

The poor wife had barely spoken a word and had spent her time trying to keep the man calm as they'd sat around the table discussing the incident. It was clear she was upset at her son's behavior but her opinion didn't seem to carry much weight in the house.

"I suppose I should be outside with them to keep an eye on things. But it's so chilly today, I wanted to stay inside where it was warm to grade my papers. I can take them home with me and do them this evening."

Grace stood up and walked toward the hooks by the door. Connor quickly caught up and took her coat down, holding it out for her to put her arms in.

She looked up at him with a grin as she did the buttons up. "You're welcome to stay and join us in a game of hide and seek."

He laughed as he opened the door to follow her outside. "I should warn you, I've always been one of the best hiders. I never get put out."

As soon as they stepped onto the front steps, the cold air hit his cheeks. He looked around at the children playing without a care in the world and wondered why they didn't seem to feel the cold at all.

He knew he really should be getting back to his shop across the street but it wouldn't hurt to spend a few more minutes here. He'd just have to stay a bit later to finish up the order he was working on today.

"Miss Hamilton! Come play with us!"

"Uncle Connor...will you push me on the swing?"

He laughed at the sudden rush of children's

voices calling out to them excitedly, wanting their attention. He walked over to Sophia who was pumping her legs to get the swing moving. With her heavy coat and boots, she was having a hard time, so he gave her a big push that sent her flying into the air. She squealed with excitement but when he looked at Grace, she had her hand on her chest and her eyes wide as she watched the little girl.

"Me too!" Another girl was on the swing on the tree next to Sophia, so he went over and pulled her back before giving her a good push forward.

Grace raced over, her eyebrows pulled together in concern. "I don't think they should be going so high. What if they fall? They could get hurt."

He leaned back against the other side of the tree, tilting his head as he glanced over at Grace. "This is coming from the girl who came across the country in a wagon with her sister, learned to ride a horse astride, helped to hide a fugitive until she could be proven innocent..."

Her mouth opened wide in shock. "You heard about that?"

He shrugged nonchalantly. "It's a small town. And, your brother is my friend. He might have mentioned your involvement in his wife's troubles when she first came to town."

Luke had filled Connor in on how he'd ended up meeting his wife, Sylvia, shortly after he'd arrived back in Bethany. And, he'd mentioned that she'd been charged with murdering the man she'd come out here to marry and Grace was convinced she was innocent. In order to buy them more time to prove it, she'd helped Sylvia escape.

And now, she was standing here worrying about him pushing a swing too high.

"Well, I hate to think what might have happened if we'd just let her be taken to face trial somewhere. No one would have believed her. So, I did what I had to do for a friend."

She shoved her hands into her pockets deeper and pulled her arms in tight as she tried to keep herself warm. Her breath hung in the air as she glanced up at the girls on the swings.

"Can you push me next, Mr. Wallace?"

Lizzie came over and tugged at his jacket. There were only the two swings, so he told her he would as soon as one of the other girls was finished.

"That's all right. I will wait my turn. I try to swing by myself but I haven't learned how to pump my legs. Oliver pushes me sometimes except he's not very strong so I don't get to go high. I want to go high like Sophia!"

"Oh, Lizzie, that's too high." Grace looked at the young girl worriedly.

He crouched down and smiled then winked at the child before whispering to her, "Don't worry, Lizzie. I'll push you as high as the top of the trees."

He knew that, to Lizzie, even a little push was going to feel like she was as high as the other girls. To her, it would be like flying.

It broke his heart knowing the poor girl didn't have anyone who could push her on the swing. That's something a pa would do and she would never have that.

Lizzie tilted her head slightly and furrowed her eyebrows together as she looked at him intently. Immediately, he tensed, preparing for what he knew was coming. It amazed him how he sometimes forgot about the scars that were visible to everyone since he'd been back home.

Being around Grace, it was easy to forget because she never seemed to notice.

"How come you have so many owies on your face?"

He swallowed, the familiar pounding in his ears as he wished things could be different. But, she was just a child and couldn't know it wasn't something she should be asking about.

"I was in a fire and it burned some of my skin."

Her little mouth opened and her eyes filled with sadness. "Does it hurt?"

Her innocent question made him smile. He didn't know if anyone had asked him if it hurt before. Usually, people just wanted to know what happened then didn't want to talk about it anymore. It was more comfortable for people to pretend they didn't see it.

"Sometimes, it does." Not just the physical scars but he didn't think the young girl needed to know anything else about it.

Suddenly, she threw her arms around his neck. "Well, I wish I could make it so it didn't hurt you anymore."

He was startled and almost fell backward as he awkwardly reached up to hug the little girl back. He didn't even know what to say.

But the gentle hug this small child offered him gave him hope that maybe, someday, the hurt could be taken away.

CHAPTER 9

Grace sat down on her front step and lifted her eyes to the sky. The moon was full tonight and it seemed to light up the large snowflakes as they slowly fell to the ground. She closed her eyes and let the cold flakes land on her cheeks as she took a deep breath of the brisk air. Everything was quiet around her as the town settled inside for the evening, the first layer of snow muffling any sound.

She always loved the first snowfall of the year when everything was so fresh and white. There was nothing better than cozying up inside by a fire during the winter months but she loved being outside to enjoy the snow on nights like this.

The crunching sound of boots on the crisp snow interrupted the silence. She opened her eyes and looked toward the street where she could see a figure walking. She squinted to see who it was and smiled when she recognized him.

Connor must have seen her sitting there, so he turned and made his way her direction, stopping and leaning against the bottom post. "Your brother would not be happy to hear you were outside past dark, you know."

She rolled her eyes at the reminder of her overprotective brother. Everyone knew how he felt about his younger sister living on her own in town.

"I sit outside many evenings and he's never found out. I'm not going to sit inside when it's so peaceful and calm out here. You're just getting finished at your shop now?" It was well past supper time so she had assumed he'd have been home long ago.

He came over and sat down on the step beside her, letting his long legs stretch out in front of him. "I wanted to finish up the job I was working on."

"It probably didn't help you coming to the school every day this week when you should have been working."

He chuckled and shrugged. "I need to have a lunch break."

"I understand now why you and my brother get along so well. You've both got this serious concern that a woman can't take care of herself."

She wasn't actually upset about Connor's lunchtime visits. She knew he was just making sure she was safe. When he'd come with her to visit with Dirk's father, he'd seen how angry the man was. And, there was a good chance the son was of a similar temperament so who knew what he could be capable of.

Trying to control some of the boys as they got older was difficult as a small woman but she'd never felt threatened by a student before. Until Dirk.

He ignored her comment and leaned back against the step above, looking up at the sky. "I'm sure the sky is nowhere near this big anywhere else in the world." A large snowflake landed on the end of his nose, so he reached up to wipe it off.

They sat in silence for a while, enjoying the quiet of the world around them. She peeked over at him, her eyes falling on the redness of his skin he so often tried to hide.

"I'm sorry for Lizzie being so inquisitive about your scars today. I know you must be tired of people asking about them."

His jaw moved as he clenched his teeth together but he kept his eyes up at the sky. She thought maybe he wasn't going to reply and she wished she hadn't even brought it up.

"She's just a child. She doesn't know any better. Besides, she didn't really say anything mean. In fact, she was probably kinder in her reaction than many adults I've come across since it happened."

He reached down and absently rubbed at his leg. She knew it bothered him a lot too, and whenever he was reminded about the scars, it seemed like he felt the pain there even more.

"I'm sorry that people can be so cruel. But, you know everyone around here sees past any scars you carry. We still see the same face who left for California all those years ago."

He laughed but she could tell there was anger behind the sound. "No one can see past them. They're there every time anyone looks at me. I know you all say you don't see them but I know that's not really possible. All I can hope is that maybe, in time, they will fade more and not be such a big part of me."

She pulled her eyebrows together in annoyance. "How can you say what I see when I look at you? Yes, I might see them physically but I mean

I see past them and they aren't what I actually see."

He looked at her, his eyes locking on hers as he shrugged. "I know you say that but, the truth is, these scars are never going away. They're going to be here for the world to see forever and there will be times when that's what you will see when you look at me. That's never going to change. It's just something I'm going to have to get used to. I've seen the way my mother's eyes look at me with sadness for the boy she misses. I've seen the pitying looks from people when they know what happened. I don't need anyone's pity."

"Connor Wallace, no one pities you, except maybe yourself."

His mouth dropped open before she looked away, not wanting him to see her anger. "We all feel bad for how you got your scars but it doesn't mean anyone pities you. It just means we care."

"Grace, you don't know what I've had to deal with after my accident. Maybe you all don't realize the way you look at me sometimes but, trust me, I see it."

She stood up, no longer wanting to sit here and talk to a man who was so determined to hold onto his own pity. She knew he'd faced difficulties and she would never likely understand it all, but she also wasn't going to let him accuse her of anything other than caring for him.

She tried to swing around to head up the steps into her house but he quickly jumped up and reached out to stop her. His hands closed around her arms and he held her still. She had no choice but to meet his eyes.

"I'm not saying it's wrong. I didn't mean to upset you but I just want you to understand."

Before she understood what was happening, his hand reached up and pushed her hair back behind her ear then his fingers slowly slid across her cheek.

His head lowered and his lips covered hers. She wanted to keep being angry with him for telling her how he believed she was feeling but her heart was already lost as the rough skin of his hand slid around her neck to pull her closer.

She gripped his coat, desperately trying to hold herself upright because she was sure her legs were going to give out beneath her.

But, as quickly as it had started, he pulled back, stepping back from her and thrusting his hand through his hair as he looked to the ground between them. She had to grab onto the rail to keep herself from falling.

"I'm sorry. I shouldn't have done that." He

turned to walk away, leaving her standing alone and suddenly feeling the coldness around her.

"How dare you! You think you can just come along and tell me how I'm feeling, then kiss me and walk away because you shouldn't have done it? Connor Wallace, I've always known you were a stubborn fool but I'm glad this happened because now I can see you never were the man I hoped you could be."

She was shaking with anger but she knew it was more than that. She was hurt. This was what she'd dreamed of for years. She'd believed ever since she first met him that he was the man she would marry.

But not anymore. If he could kiss her, then push her away and say it was a mistake, then she didn't want anything more to do with him.

She now realized he wasn't the same boy she'd fallen for when she was a little girl. They'd both grown up and he was dealing with issues he wasn't prepared to let go of.

So, for her own sake, she was letting him go from her heart. She couldn't keep doing this.

It was time to move on and live her life without waiting for him.

CHAPTER 10

G race walked quickly, pulling the collar of her thick coat up higher around her cheeks as the cool breeze stung her skin. The snow crunched loudly under her feet as she came around the corner by O'Hara's Mercantile. She had decided to enjoy her Saturday by baking today while the weather was too cold to be outside.

After speaking with Connor last night, she was determined to find something to keep her mind busy and forget the stubborn man even existed.

So, she was going to make some cookies to take over to Sylvia later. Hopefully, her brother's wife would be feeling well enough to enjoy them.

It would be nice to have a visit with her friend and talk about something other than Connor.

As she got closer, she could see two children sitting on the bench outside.

"Lizzie? Oliver? What are you both doing out here?"

The little girl lifted a tear-soaked face and jumped up to wrap her arms around Grace's legs. "Oh, Miss Hamilton. We have to go away. I'll never see you ever again."

Grace tried to understand what the child was saying but she wasn't quite sure she was hearing things right. She looked at Oliver, pulling her eyebrows together in confusion as she pulled Lizzie along beside her, and sat down between the children.

"What is going on, Oliver?"

The boy's eyes were wet but he was fighting the tears. He quickly looked away, staring down at the snowy ground by his feet. "Our grandma says she just can't look after us anymore. It's too hard, with her arthritis." He glanced back up, his sad eyes meeting hers. "I've tried real hard to help around the house, and with Lizzie. I've tried to do what a man would do and keep us from being a burden but Grandma says she just can't do it."

Grace's heart started pounding. If their

grandma couldn't look after them, where would they go? She was sure she'd heard at the time their parents died that they had no other family.

"I'm sure this is just some kind of misunderstanding. Where is your grandma now, Oliver?"

He tilted his head toward the mercantile. "She went in there. We're waiting for the lawyer to arrive. Then once they figure everything out, he's going to escort us to the orphanage in Oregon City in a few days."

Her heart dropped into her stomach. What could she possibly say to these children that would make them feel better? They had no one except their grandmother and, now, they were being sent away to a life no child could want.

"You children stay right here. I'm going to go in and talk to your grandmother. Maybe you've just got things confused." Grace stood up and started toward the steps.

Lizzie's eyes were wide as she lifted her head. "Miss Hamilton, will you be able to get our grandma to change her mind? So we can stay here?"

"I'm not sure I can do anything, Lizzie, but I need to see what is going on. Just stay right here."

She couldn't make any promises when she was still in shock over what she'd just heard. She knew

Mrs. Harvey did struggle with her ailments and taking on the responsibility of two young children had been hard on her. Her husband had died a few years prior and she was left to survive on her own out here by renting out her small bit of farmland.

The bell above the door rang loudly, announcing her entry. She noticed Susan O'Hara was on this side of the counter with her arm around the shoulder of the other woman. Mrs. Harvey had her head in her hands and Susan looked toward Grace with sorrow.

"Mrs. Harvey, I just spoke with the children outside. Is there anything I can do to help you?" She quickly went over and offered another arm of comfort to the older woman.

The woman lifted her head and shook it sadly. Immediately, Grace noticed the tiredness behind her eyes. She was heartbroken but she knew she just had no other choice. Her tattered bonnet reminded Grace of how this poor woman had given everything she had to feed and clothe two children she loved but it wasn't fair to ask it of her at her age. She barely had enough for herself to survive.

"I've spoken with the orphanage in Oregon City and they're sending a lawyer down here at the beginning of the week. We'll discuss everything and I need to make sure I know the children will be taken good care of before I sign anything. I've asked him to stay here a few days to give them a chance to get used to the idea and to be comfortable with him before the trip to the orphanage. It breaks my heart but I just can't do it anymore."

Her words broke in a sob and she put her head back down in her hands.

"Is there no other family or anyone who could take them, Mrs. Harvey? You've done your best and no one can blame you for not being able to shoulder the extra burden."

The woman sniffed, lifting a tissue to wipe delicately at her nose. "No, there's no other family. I'm their only kin. And, I don't know who else would be able to take them in. It's a lot to ask for someone to take on the responsibility of two children when it seems everyone is struggling to just survive without two extra mouths to feed." She swallowed and looked down at her shaking hands. "No, this is for the best. They're just such good children. I wish I could have done more for them."

Grace's eyes met Susan's over the other woman's downturned head. Susan shook her head sadly, unsure what they could possibly say to help.

Grace turned slightly, seeing the backs of the children sitting on the bench by the steps. They were huddled together and she could see Oliver was talking to his sister, likely trying to be strong and telling her they would be fine.

"Can they come live with me?"

The words were out of her mouth before she'd even thought it through. But seeing those children, and knowing they had no one who could help them, tore at her soul. Grace knew how hard it was to lose both parents and to be left to face the world without them.

But, she was lucky to have had a sister and a brother who were old enough to take care of her.

If not for them, Grace would have faced the same fate as Oliver and Lizzie.

Both of the women stared at her in shock. Truthfully, Grace was feeling just as shocked and didn't know where the idea had even come from.

"But, Grace, you're barely more than a child yourself." Mrs. Harvey shook her head. "It would be too much for you."

Hearing someone tell her she couldn't do it made her even more determined. "Well, I had my eighteenth birthday last month and, to be fair, I've been teaching children in my care for a year now. My sister Phoebe was my age when she brought me across the country to Oregon. So, I don't see why I can't take on the care of two children who need a home."

Mrs. Harvey looked toward Susan, who smiled at Grace. "I've known Grace Hamilton since we came across the country on that wagon train and, I can tell you, there's likely not another woman as tough as she is. If she says she can handle taking two children into her home to raise, I have no doubt she can do it."

The older woman looked back at Grace, a spark of hope starting to reflect in her eyes. "But, you're not married. I don't know if it would even be allowed."

"Why wouldn't it be allowed? They let the children be left in your care as a widow. And, they're under your guardianship. Surely, it's up to you to decide where the children go to live."

"I don't know. I would have to speak with the lawyer and see what we could do. I'm almost afraid to get my hopes up. If the children could stay here in Bethany, it would make me so happy. I could still see them and know they were taken care of." She reached out and took both of

Grace's hands in hers. "Are you sure? It's a lot of responsibility."

Grace nodded and gently squeezed the trembling hands. She knew in her heart how sure she was even if she hadn't really had time to think everything through.

"Let's see what the lawyer says before we say anything to anyone else, especially the children. I'd hate to get their hopes up if it's already out of our hands."

As Grace looked back out the window at the huddled figures on the bench, she knew it wasn't only the children she wanted to keep from getting their hopes up.

Somehow, she had started to hope for something she would never have imagined when she woke up this morning.

And she was determined to make it happen.

CHAPTER 11

"Daddy, you should have seen how high Uncle Connor pushed me! I saw over the trees! And he pushed all my friends too."

Connor grinned at his brother while they listened to Sophia tell all about the fun she'd had on the swing at the school this past week. She'd been telling her father every detail of the fun she'd had with her uncle coming over to the school every day.

He was enjoying the job of being the favorite uncle to all of the nieces and nephews since he'd been back in town. Ever since they'd arrived at Reid and Audrey's after church today, it seemed like all of the children were taking turns wanting his attention.

Reid leaned back in his chair and tilted his

head to the side. "That's funny, I didn't even know Uncle Connor was still going to school."

Sophia giggled as she hopped down from his lap. "No, he doesn't go to school, silly. He's too old for that. He just comes to visit us every day."

Connor ignored the look his brother was giving him and pretended to be focusing on the other children playing on the floor over by the fireplace.

"Really? That's sure nice of him to go over and visit you every day."

"Well, he doesn't just visit me. He spends a lot of time with Miss Hamilton too."

"Oh, does he?"

He wasn't going to give Reid the satisfaction of seeing the smug look he knew would be on his brother's face. Especially since now, after what happened the other evening in front of her house, Connor was quite certain Grace would kick him straight out the door if he showed up at the school again.

She'd been polite today as the family gathered to visit briefly outside of church but he suspected it was only because other people were around them. Then, she'd declined to come out for the after-church gathering, saying she had a lot of papers to grade before tomorrow.

Grace wasn't one to pass up a visit with family, so he knew it was because of him.

He finally turned to face his brother as Sophia ran over to play with the twins who were calling her name. Reid had a smirk on his face that made Connor want to kick him off his chair. But, they were grown men now so it wasn't like he could act like he might have when they were younger.

"Before you start thinking anything that really isn't any of your concern anyway, I'm simply going over to the school during the lunch break to put wood in the stove and to make sure that Dirk kid doesn't cause any trouble for Grace. That's all it is. I've known Grace a long time so I'm just looking out for her."

"Oh, of course. I'm sure that's all it is. I mean, she barely survived in the year she's been teaching there, so it's good that you're here now to help."

Connor rolled his eyes and clenched his jaw. He looked around hopefully, seeing if anyone was around who could interrupt this conversation. But it seemed like the one time he wished for the chaos that was usually around them when the family was together, there was no one even paying any attention to them.

"It doesn't matter anyway. Grace is likely a bit

upset with me, so I'm not sure I'll be hanging around there much, at least for a while."

Why did he even tell his brother anything? He could already see the questions in Reid's eyes before he even spoke.

"What did you do to make Grace mad at you?"

Connor's mouth fell open. "Why do you automatically assume I did something wrong?"

"Because I know you. And I know Grace is just about the sweetest, most forgiving, kindest woman in the entire country. So, if she's upset with you, I can guarantee it's your own fault."

Connor stared at his brother in disbelief. Even though he knew deep down every word Reid said was true, he really didn't feel like letting him know it.

"I didn't do anything more than tell Grace the truth about any expectations she might have for more between us than it could ever be."

Now Reid rolled his eyes dramatically as he shook his head. "Connor, give it up. You've got to stop making excuses." He put his hand up before Connor could interrupt him. "No, you're going to listen to me. As the oldest brother, it's up to me to sometimes knock some sense into the others whether they like it or not. And since Ma wouldn't be too happy with me if I actually did knock you on the head like I'd like to do, I'm going to make you listen to me."

Right now, Connor would much rather his brother did try hitting him. At least he wouldn't have to listen to him.

"I remember a few years ago, just before you headed off on your grand adventures, and we were sitting outside under a tree after church. I'd been hurting for a long time after losing my wife and worrying about how I'd raise Sophia on my own. My youngest brother, who wasn't even really a man yet, pointed out to me how stubborn I was being and not seeing something right in front of my eyes."

Connor searched his memory for what his brother was talking about.

"That day, after you planted the seed, I realized I had to take a chance. If not for you pushing me, I might never have married Audrey." Reid looked over at his wife who was talking with Phoebe. Connor could see the love in his brother's eyes in that simple look. "I would never have known the love I have now and I can't even imagine how my life would have gone."

Reid turned back to face him. "So, if that young boy could point his older brother in the right direction, I'd say it's a pretty good chance that now I can return the favor. Don't be stupid and throw something away just because you're hung up on some perceived issues that would keep you from being worthy of someone like Grace."

Connor swallowed, not sure how his brother could understand so much without him ever telling him all of it.

But, the truth was, no one knew all of the story. They didn't know what else he'd lost that day after the fire. It still tore at him and left him feeling like he had nothing to offer any woman, especially one as perfect as Grace.

"What you and Audrey have is wonderful and I see it with all of you. Do you think I don't look around and wish I could have what all of my siblings and friends have found? But it's different for me. Look at me. I'm not the same as you all are and that's the truth."

Reid's jaw was clenched tightly and Connor could see the muscles moving as he struggled to keep his temper under control. After their pa had died when Connor was just a boy, Reid had stepped into the role as his father and Connor respected him more than anyone in the world.

But he wasn't sure he could take his advice this time.

"The only one who doesn't see you the same as the rest of us is you and you need to get over that. Before you lose the one chance to have what you just said you wished you could have."

Reid stood up, obviously done trying to get through to him. Connor wished he could tell his brother everything else but the shame and humiliation still cut him deep.

But, he was willing to admit, Reid's words had somehow managed to give him something to think about. And, something he hadn't had in a very long time.

Hope that maybe, it was just a bit possible, he could have more.

CHAPTER 12

"You must be Grace Hamilton. My name is Henry Willard. Mrs. Harvey has sent me over here to speak with you about the children."

Grace stood up from behind her desk, smoothing her skirt out as she walked forward to meet the man who'd walked into the school. She'd been waiting for him since school was let out today knowing he would be coming.

She'd spoken with Mrs. Harvey after church yesterday and she'd mentioned he would be arriving today so she would ask him to meet with her.

"It's nice to meet you, Mr. Willard."

The lawyer was not at all what she'd been expecting. For some reason, she'd assumed he would be an older, short, balding man. That's what most of the lawyers she'd met over the years looked like.

But this man was likely closer to her brother's age. And he was certainly not short or balding. As he took his hat off to greet her, she noticed his thick brown hair that was combed back neatly. He smiled at her warmly.

"Well, I understand you have an interest in taking over care of the Harvey children. The matter of guardianship can be complicated, especially as the process of admission into the system with the orphanage has already been started, but I'd be happy to discuss what possible options might be available."

"I just thought since the guardian is willing to let the children come live with me instead of the orphanage, it would be a simple matter of her signing them over to me."

Grace knew it wasn't perhaps going to be as easy as that even if she had hoped it somehow could be.

"Oh, there are many things that need to be considered. I suppose if Mrs. Harvey had just asked you to take the children without contacting us, it might have made things a bit easier. But, I would be neglecting my duties if I didn't ensure the placement of the children was in their best interests."

"Absolutely, that's what I want for the children too. So, just tell me what I need to do."

The lawyer pulled his coat up tighter around his chin and looked around the cold room they were standing in. Grace hadn't wanted to stoke the fire too much as it was the end of the day and she knew she'd be leaving soon.

"Would you be able to join me at the boardinghouse for a meal? I'm afraid I've been traveling most of the day and I'm quite hungry. I've already dropped all of my baggage off in my room and the smell of the roast beef Mrs. Larsen was cooking has consumed my thoughts."

Grace walked over to take her coat off the hook and let the man help her get it over her shoulders. "Thank you, Mr. Willard. Mrs. Larsen is the best cook in town, so I'd love to join you."

"Oh, please. Call me Henry. I reserve my more formal name for business only."

Grace had a moment of discomfort, wondering what he meant since she'd assumed what they were going to be discussing was business. But, she also appreciated that he was a handsome man so if he did have any other interest in her, she would be foolish to ignore it.

One thing she'd decided since her talk with Connor the other night was that she wasn't sitting around and waiting for life to come to her anymore. She didn't care if she never married or if she met someone and fell head over heels in love with them tomorrow. Whatever happened, happened and she was just going to enjoy what she couldn't control and take what she could into her own hands.

Including the possibility of raising two children on her own.

They made their way outside, the cool air hitting her cheeks. The snow from the other night still covered the ground and, as they started up the street toward the boardinghouse, Henry put his arm out to allow her to loop hers through. She welcomed the assistance because the boots she wore were quite slippery sometimes and the last thing she wanted to do when trying to impress this man into letting her have the children was to fall down on her face in front of him.

"Bethany is a nice little town. I'm used to life in the city but I do travel quite often around the area and admit I sometimes enjoy the slower pace of a smaller community."

"Yes, Bethany is a wonderful place to live. It

might not have the excitement of the city but you have everything you could need."

As they walked past Connor's shop, Grace saw him coming outside to close up for the day. She was thankful they were already on their way and on the other side of the street so they didn't actually bump into him.

They made it to the boardinghouse and Henry held the door open to let her inside. "Hello, Mrs. Larsen. Would we be able to get a table for supper?"

She wanted to be sitting in the dining room before Connor came in behind them, so she sighed with relief when they were seated right away. Now, she just had to hope he went straight up to his room and didn't come to eat for a bit. "It's so nice to have you here this evening, Grace. And you too, Mr. Willard. I've done a nice roast beef for supper."

Bethany didn't have a real cafe other than the saloon which they opened up for everyone during the day to be used as an eating establishment. Grace quite often ate here, sometimes on her own, or else joining Sylvia and Luke. Her stomach suddenly churned with worry. What if they decided to show up today? How would she explain being here with a lawyer?

She already knew Connor had seen them and she was sure Dorothy Larsen had questions about it too. But, right now, Grace just wanted to focus on discussing the children. She would worry about what to tell everyone later.

The door to the dining room opened as Mrs. Larsen went to get them some tea to drink while waiting for their food. Connor walked in and scowled in her direction before taking a seat at a table across from her.

Of all people she didn't want in this room distracting her right now, he had to sit right there. She moved over slightly, hoping Henry would be able to block her somewhat from the eyes boring into her.

"So, Miss Hamilton..."

She interrupted him, giving him a warm smile. "Please, call me Grace."

The corners of his mouth curled as he nodded. "Grace. So, are you sure you've thought through the ramifications of taking on the care of two children? I know you're still a young woman and Mrs. Harvey mentioned you're not married."

Her heart lurched. She'd truly hoped that wouldn't make a difference, but she knew she was being overly optimistic. In today's world, a woman wasn't deemed as capable of taking care of herself as a man could. And, that would likely be the same with children too.

If they weren't kin, it might not be as easy as she'd hoped for someone else to take guardianship.

"No, I'm not married at this time. However, I do make a wage by teaching at the school. So I'm certain I'd be able to provide for the children with everything they could need."

She hoped her voice sounded more sure than she was feeling inside. She knew it was going to be hard but she was willing to take on other jobs if she had to in order to provide for Oliver and Lizzie. Grace wasn't going to sit around and wait for a husband to take care of them.

"Well, it does make things a bit more complicated but I'm hopeful we can ensure you have some kind of guardianship of the children until such a time they can find something more permanent."

Grace's brows pulled together in confusion. "What do you mean, more permanent?"

Mrs. Larsen came and set their food down on the table and Grace caught Connor's eye as Henry moved slightly to grab a napkin. He didn't look like he'd moved since he sat down, but he had a steaming cup of coffee in front of him and he slowly brought it up to his lips.

She brought her eyes back to Henry's. "Oh, well, I mean until we could possibly find a permanent adopter for the children. There are some people looking for older children, especially young boys who can help on farms."

She shook her head slowly. "I'm sorry but I think you've misunderstood. I'm planning to take the children permanently. I want to adopt them."

The lawyer was about to take a bite but he lowered his fork back to his plate.

"Oh. This does possibly make things a bit more complicated."

Her heart sunk. "Does that mean you don't think it's possible?"

He took a bite, chewing slowly. His eyes closed briefly as he savored every bite, leaving her annoyed at having to wait for his answer.

Finally, he swallowed and dabbed at his lips with his napkin. "No, it's not impossible. Just a bit more difficult. But, lucky for you, I enjoy a challenge. It just means I might have to stick around Bethany a few more days while we work out all the details. You're just going to have to put up with me a little longer, I'm afraid."

She wanted to throw her arms around him and

hug him if it meant he was going to try and help her. Instead, she laughed, letting go of some of the worry she'd been holding in.

If he was willing to make it possible for her to adopt those children, she was willing to put up with just about anything.

CHAPTER 13

Connor slammed his hammer down onto the hot steel, sparks flying toward his leather apron as he lifted his arm to bring it down again. One of the things he'd always loved about his work was the chance to bang his frustrations and anger out on the heated metal he was shaping.

Beads of sweat formed on his forehead from the heat inside the building. Usually, he would take regular breaks to step outside for fresh air and to cool himself down a bit but, today, he was enjoying the punishment of staying inside to face the heat.

Plus, he didn't want to take any chances of stepping outside and seeing Grace. Or, more specifically, Grace with that man.

Connor had been shocked to see her walking out of the school with the man yesterday and then sitting down for a meal with him at the boardinghouse. He didn't know why he'd followed them in to eat instead of just continuing up to his room like he should have done.

But, he'd forced himself to sit there, even though the longer he'd stayed, the angrier he'd become.

The man was immaculately dressed, with a long dress coat worn over top of a nice suit. The kind of suit Connor usually only wore to funerals.

It was obvious the man was wealthy and it irked him to see that he was the kind of man who would surely turn any woman's head. He had sat watching them laugh and talk during their meal until they were finished and the man had escorted Grace over to her house.

Mrs. Larsen had told him the man was a lawyer who was in town on business. Exactly the kind of man Grace deserved to have courting her.

Connor had stepped outside earlier, thinking he would go across to check on things at the school like he'd been doing before his fight with Grace, even knowing he wouldn't likely be welcomed, but had stopped short when he saw the man going up the steps to the school again today.

He brought his hammer down again, trying to knock the memory from his mind of Grace meeting him at the door with a smile and welcoming him inside.

He wasn't sure if he was more angry with Grace for showing an interest in another man or himself for caring about it so much. He was the one who'd made it clear to her nothing would happen between them.

"If you keep banging on that piece of metal, there'll be nothing left to it."

Connor jumped at the sound of Luke's voice behind him. He spun around to see the other man leaning against the workbench.

"I didn't hear you come in."

"I kind of figured. The way you were pounding on that hot metal, I imagine a herd of bison could have ran through here without you noticing."

Connor pulled his gloves off then reached up and wiped the wetness from his brow. "You always have a knack with exaggerating. I'm sure if you'd announced your entry, I'd have heard you just fine."

Luke just shrugged and laughed. "Well, I was

going to let you know I was here but didn't know if I'd be heard above the racket you were making anyway."

"Is there something I can help you with?"

Connor really wasn't in the mood to make small talk with Grace's brother even if he was a good friend.

"I was going to see if you could make me a shovel to use around back where we get up to our living quarters. I'm worried about Sylvia with the snow. She's having so much trouble getting around now. The baby is going to be here any day and I don't need to worry about her slipping and falling. If she'd just stay home when I'm not around, it wouldn't be such a worry, but she doesn't listen to common sense."

"Is she feeling any better?"

Luke shook his head. "She's had such a hard time. I hate seeing her like this. I just hope when the baby decides to come, she won't have any trouble."

Connor watched the worry cross his friend's face and he felt guilty for his earlier annoyance with him. The worries Luke was facing were more concerning than his own.

"I'm sure everything will be fine. When the

time comes, if you need me to ride out to get the doctor, just let me know."

"I'd appreciate that. Grace is going to be there to help and Susan O'Hara has said she will come. She's helped deliver a lot of babies over the years. So, hopefully, we won't have any need for the doctor."

Connor walked over and set his hammer on the workbench by Luke, then went to the back of the shop where he kept the scraps of metal. "I can have that done for you by tonight so you can get the pathway cleared up. You don't need to be worrying about Sylvia."

When he turned back around holding the piece of metal he'd chosen, he almost ran into Luke who'd followed him.

"So, now are you going to tell me what's got you so bothered? I've known you long enough to see something's eating at you."

Connor pushed past him and went back to the workbench. "Nothing that concerns you. You've got your own things to be thinking about."

Luke chuckled, then put his hands up in fake surrender when Connor turned to glare at him. "Sorry, I didn't mean to pry. Just that I have my suspicions, considering how ornery my sister was when I spoke to her Saturday morning, then she decided not to go out to the farm after church on Sunday. I figured with the pair of you both being in similar tempers, something must have happened."

"Again, nothing that concerns you. Your sister is a friend of mine, nothing more than that. You should be more worried about the man she's been hanging around with and having meals with in the evenings."

Now, he had Luke's full attention and he enjoyed knowing he'd shocked his friend. Served him right for prying into his business anyway.

"What man? What are you talking about?"

"Well, that's something you're going to have to ask your sister about."

Luke was already heading to the doorway and Connor couldn't help grinning to himself. At least if he couldn't say anything to her about how she was carrying on with some strange man, she would have to listen to her brother.

But, as Luke threw the door open, Sylvia was standing there and he almost knocked her over.

"Luke, I'm not feeling well. I think it's time."

All of his earlier anger at Grace was gone in that moment and, as his friend looked back at him with a panicked expression, Connor could only hope that everything would go all right for both the woman and baby.

"I'll go tell Grace. We'll be there shortly."

He knew if there was a need for the doctor, he had to be close by to make the ride to get him. So, Grace was just going to have to put her anger at him aside long enough for them to be there together.

And he figured since they would likely have some time while they waited, then it likely wouldn't hurt for him to ask her a few questions.

CHAPTER 14

"Grace, I'm so scared. What if something goes wrong?"

Grace sat on the edge of the bed, facing Sylvia as she patted a cold cloth on her friend's forehead. She reached down and squeezed her hand, offering her a brave smile.

"Sylvia, don't think like that. You're strong. Just think of everything you've been through. Luke is here and I know he's not going to let anything happen to you. Or the baby."

Grace wished she could promise her friend the words she spoke, but she knew there was no way she could know everything was going to be all right. Sylvia had been in so much pain now for hours and nothing was happening. Susan and Luke were out in the other room, letting the girls have some time alone while they had something to eat.

Connor had left well over an hour ago to get the doctor. But it had started snowing again and was coming down hard, so it would be wet, cold and hard to see as he rode to the next town over for the only doctor in the area.

Grace just hoped he could find him and bring him here on time.

Sylvia let out a loud cry, then squeezed Grace's hand until she was sure there would be broken bones when she let go. She stood up, holding tightly to her friend's hand as she helped talk her through the painful contraction.

Luke came in and rushed over to the side of the bed. He took Sylvia's other hand, then looked across at Grace. She gave him a hopeful smile. "She's doing great. The baby will be here soon, I'm sure of it."

"Has Connor come back with the doctor yet?" Sylvia's voice was weak, showing her exhaustion.

"Not yet, but he'll be here any minute now."

Thankfully, as soon as he said the words, they heard the outside door slam. Within seconds, Susan was coming into the room with the doctor in tow.

Grace gave a sigh of relief, before leaning in

and squeezing her friend's hand. "I'll just be in the other room. I can't wait to meet the baby."

Sylvia smiled but her eyes reflected the pain and fear that was still so real to her.

Grace walked out of the bedroom, leaving Luke and Susan inside with the doctor to help with the delivery. As she closed the door behind her, she closed her eyes and leaned back against it, finally taking a moment to let her own worries overcome her. She'd been trying to put on a brave face for the others but, the truth was, she'd never seen anyone in as much pain as Sylvia was all day.

Grace was terrified something was going to go wrong.

"How's she doing?"

Her eyes opened and she noticed Connor still standing by the doorway, his coat soaked through from the snow and his hair hanging limply around his red face. He'd been out in this freezing weather to get the doctor and, in that moment, she couldn't have been more thankful he was here.

"She's having a hard time. But, she's strong, so I'm sure she'll be all right." She walked over by the stove and set the coffee pot back on top. "Let me make you some coffee so you can get warmed up. I'm sure you're almost frozen all the way through."

He shrugged his coat off and set it over the back of a chair before sitting down. "The snow is sure coming down. And when I got there, the doctor was at a farm just outside of town so I had to go out and find him. I was afraid we wouldn't make it back in time. Thankfully, he was willing to saddle up a horse to ride back with me so we could make better time. If he'd insisted on bringing his carriage, I think I would have had to knock some sense into him."

The middle-aged doctor was known for his fancy carriage he drove as he made his rounds in the area. It made it easy to spot him and to find him if you needed him. All you had to do was look for the carriage.

She poured him his coffee, then sat across from him, letting her head drop into her hands as they heard Sylvia's moans from the other room.

"She'll be okay, Grace. You said yourself how tough she is. Some women just have a harder time than others. The doctor is in there now, so he will take care of her."

She lifted her head, the light from the only lantern in the room illuminating the table between them. He smiled at her reassuringly before taking a sip of his coffee. As he brought it to his lips, he started sputtering and choking. He quickly set the cup down then lifted his fingers to his mouth. "Ouch, that's still hot."

Grace had to laugh and welcomed the chance to have a break from the worry on her heart. "Of course it is. I just took it off the stove."

He looked at her with a pained expression, his fingers still pressed to his lips. A piercing scream broke the silence and Grace jumped to her feet, wanting to run into the other room and help her friend.

But she knew there was nothing she could do. It was all up to the doctor and the others who were in there with her. Grace had never felt so helpless in her life. Just when she was sure she was going to collapse from the heaviness of everything happening, Connor came over and pulled her into him, wrapping his arms around her.

She let him give her his strength as she clung to him, burying her head in his shoulder. He cupped a hand to the back of her head, holding her close. She could hear every beat of his heart as she let the tears finally flow. In that moment, she needed him to keep her standing because she was sure she had nothing else in her to give.

They stood like that for what seemed like an

eternity, their breathing the only sounds between them.

When she finally felt like she could stand on her own, she slowly pulled back, keeping her head down so he couldn't see the wetness on her cheeks. She was suddenly embarrassed, unsure what to say.

He brought his hand under her chin and forced her to look up at him. "It's going to be okay."

The sureness in his words and reflected in his eyes made her believe him. She knew he couldn't promise it any more than she could but, for some reason, the words calmed her fears.

She swallowed, pulling away to walk back toward the table, bringing her arms up to hug herself against the sudden chill that gripped her after being wrapped in his arms.

"Do you want some more coffee?" She had to break the awkwardness she suddenly felt.

He laughed as he came over and sat back in his chair. "No, I still can't swallow this one without causing pain, so I'll just wait for it to cool off a bit."

She smiled at him, sitting down and absently letting her eyes go back to the door that was between her and her friend. They sat in silence for a while listening to the wind beating against the window. At least it seemed like Sylvia was having a break in her pain as the noise in the other room stopped.

"So, I should warn you that, once the baby arrives safely and everyone is feeling better, your brother might have some questions for you. I just thought you should be prepared."

Grace turned to look at him. He had his hands cupped around his warm mug as he watched her.

"What do you mean? What kind of questions?"

He looked down at his coffee and she almost thought he seemed embarrassed or uncomfortable about what he was bringing up. What was he talking about?

"Just about the man you've been seen around town with."

He kept his eyes down while she sat with her mouth wide open. Was he seriously trying to find out who the man was she'd been seen with?

She had to fight the urge to grab the cup of coffee from his hands and throw it in his face.

"Well, he can go ahead and ask me. It's really no one's business but my own."

He finally looked at her and she pretended she

didn't see the pain that flashed in his eyes. "Who is he, Grace? You really shouldn't just be hanging around strange men without anyone else knowing who he is."

Her heart pounded with anger. How dare he think he had any right to know who the man was? She enjoyed a moment of knowing he was jealous. He deserved it.

And she was going to enjoy telling him the truth about who he was even more. Because she knew that what she was about to tell him would leave him unable to say another word to her.

"Well, not that it's any of your business but Henry is a lawyer from Oregon City. He's a very nice man and, quite frankly, I've enjoyed spending time with him. He's made it clear he enjoys my company too. But, while he's here, he's been helping me get everything in order to adopt Oliver and Lizzie."

Connor's mouth opened but he didn't say a word. Finally, he shook his head slightly, bringing his eyebrows together. "You're not serious."

"Oh, I'm very serious. They need someone to take them in and give them a home. They need someone who can love them. I can do that for them."

"But how? How do you think you're going to

raise two children by yourself? Grace, you need to think this through. I know you sometimes let your emotions get ahead of you but raising children isn't easy. You can't do it."

Anger filled her as she glared at him. "I *can* do it. And, while it would make things a lot easier for the adoption to go through if I weren't a single woman, Henry has assured me he will do everything he can to make it happen. He's been a great help to me. He's a good man and I'm glad to have him on my side."

She knew she was being mean by adding that last part in, especially since she'd never really given Connor or anyone else the chance to help her with it, but she didn't care. Right now, she wanted to hurt him.

She wanted to hurt him for hurting her.

Suddenly, a loud scream came from the other room, followed shortly by the sound of a baby crying.

She jumped up, racing to the door that opened to show her brother standing there holding a baby, a wide grin covering his face.

"It's a boy! Meet your nephew, Joseph."

As she took the baby into her arms, tears of relief and love flowing down her face, she looked up to see Connor standing to the side. He looked like he'd just been punched in the stomach but she didn't care.

This boy in her arms helped her know in her heart she was doing the right thing for those children even if Connor, her brother, or anyone else tried to tell her she couldn't do it.

Every child deserved someone to love them. And she was determined to be that someone for Lizzie and Oliver.

CHAPTER 15

C onnor pushed another piece of wood into the stove opening, letting it catch before closing the grate. He rubbed his hands together in front of the heat, allowing the warmth to seep into his fingers. The wind had died down slightly from yesterday, and the snow had let up, but it was cold outside and inside the small school room wasn't much warmer.

He'd made sure he was up earlier than normal to be here in plenty of time to get the fire going. It was a routine he'd been doing all last week but hadn't done it yesterday because of the fight he'd had with Grace.

Today, though, he'd been determined he would be here to do it and, hopefully, have the chance to talk to her before the children arrived for the day.

Guilt had eaten at him all night after he'd gone home. He knew he shouldn't have brought up the subject of the other man Grace had been seeing, especially during a time when she was obviously distraught and worried. But, he'd never been known for doing things the right way and he'd proven that last night.

After he'd held her in his arms, letting her lean into him while she let go of the stress of what was happening around them, he couldn't get his mind off his jealousy.

He knew that's what it was. Complete jealousy over what he'd thought was happening with Grace and that other man. Even though he'd told her nothing would ever happen with him, he'd obviously never thought through what that would mean.

Because the thought of her being with anyone else killed him.

"Connor, what are you doing here? I told you, I don't need you starting the fire for me in the morning. I'm capable of coming in early enough to get the school warmed up before the children get here."

He stood up and faced Grace as she walked inside, closing the door softly behind her.

"I know but I have to go in and get the fires

going in my shop early so it's no trouble for me to come over here and start one for you."

For some reason, he felt like a young boy who had been caught doing something he wasn't supposed to be doing. He stepped back and let her get past him to her desk, then followed her as she placed her books down.

"I just wanted to apologize for bringing up my concerns with the lawyer. I honestly had no idea who he was and was just worried for your safety, that's all. I didn't mean to pry."

She stood behind her desk, her hands resting on the books. She lifted her eyes to his and he was struck at the blueness once more. Sometimes, her eyes seemed bluer than the sky and it would take his breath away.

"Well, now that you know who he is, you don't need to worry."

He knew she was hurt and angry with him but he wasn't sure what he could say to make things better between them.

"No, I guess not. But, I admit I'm a bit worried about whether or not you've completely thought through adopting two children on your own." As soon as he said the words, he knew he'd made things worse. Her cheeks reddened with anger and he'd known Grace long enough to know she was about to put him in his place.

"Connor, I appreciate your concern over my life, however, you have no right to question anything. You have made it clear to me that there is no future between us and, quite frankly, what I do now with my life is absolutely no business of yours."

He clenched his jaw tight, knowing everything she said was true, but not prepared to give up. If he was being completely honest, he wasn't sure why he was so concerned, especially when she was right. None of this was any of his concern.

"Grace, I care about you. I've known you a long time. I just want to make sure you've thought things through. It's a big commitment and not something you can do on a whim."

Her eyes narrowed and she walked around her desk toward him. "I'm not doing this on a whim. Maybe it's a bit sudden but the circumstances for these children didn't leave much time for waiting. They need a home and, if I'm allowed, I'm going to give that to them."

He pushed his fingers through his hair. "Well then, I think we should get married."

Her mouth dropped open and the fire crackling in the stove sounded louder than cannon shots in the silence of the room.

She shook her head slowly, her eyes filled with sadness. "Ever since I was a little girl, I hoped I would hear those words from you, Connor. And a week ago, I had dared to hope maybe it was something that could happen. But not now. You don't want to marry me out of love. You're only doing it because you're like all the other men in my life who don't think I can handle this on my own." She turned and walked away from him, going to stand by the window.

The sun was peeking over the horizon, giving her skin an orange glow as she looked outside. "I will never marry a man who is settling for me or marrying me out of some sense of obligation."

How could he make her understand? It wasn't his fault he was pushing her away. He was doing it for her because he knew she'd end up regretting her feelings for him.

"Grace, I just thought that by marrying me, it would make things easier for you to be approved for the adoption. I'm just trying to help because I can see how important this is to you. I do think you can handle it on your own. I have no doubt about that at all. But, if it would help you, then I was offering what I could to make it happen."

Connor had never been so confused in his life. He knew he was just making things worse between him and Grace and the last thing he wanted to do was hurt her.

He'd never planned to ask her to marry him. But, now, he realized how much he'd hoped she would say yes. Asking her this way had been his chance to do it without putting his heart on the line. He'd used the excuse of wanting to help her when the truth was, he'd hoped with everything he had that she would say yes.

It seemed like every time he opened his mouth to speak, he said something wrong.

"I think you should go. Right now, it's best if you just stay away from me for a while. I need to focus on getting Lizzie and Oliver and building a home for them. And you're just making things harder for me. For whatever reason, I've never been the girl you wanted. You've always known how I felt about you because my heart was on my sleeve. But I've never been good enough and I can't do it anymore. So, please, just leave me alone."

Before he could say anything more to her, the doors opened and the first few children made their way inside. The sounds of their cheerful laughter as they took their coats off and greeted

Miss Hamilton were at odds with the dark sadness Connor was feeling in his heart.

"Hi Mr. Wallace. Look at the nice marble my brother gave me. Isn't it pretty?" He looked down at the shiny round piece of glass Lizzie held out for him to see.

"It's very pretty, Lizzie. You're a lucky girl."

"Well, we have to go to an orphanage so I guess my brother is trying to cheer me up. I don't want to leave here because I'm scared and I will miss everyone. But, I'll be okay. Oliver says he will look after me."

Connor realized they must not have told the children about any possibility of living with Grace in case it didn't happen.

Suddenly, he felt horrible knowing he'd ever questioned what she was doing. He knew she was doing the right thing and he hoped she would be able to do it.

These kids deserved a woman like Grace to love them.

When he got to the door, he looked back and his eyes locked with hers. And he realized with a tightening in his chest that he had never deserved the love she'd offered to him.

CHAPTER 16

"Oh, Sylvia. He's precious. I can't believe how much a person can love someone so new to the world." Grace's heart swelled as she held the swaddled baby in her arms. He slept soundly, his little lips moving every now and then as he cooed in his sleep.

"He is the most precious baby in the world but I guess I could be a bit biased." Sylvia smiled over at her, then looked at Luke. "We've been truly blessed. This boy will never be short of love."

"You sure did cause your mommy and daddy a lot of worry, little man. Not to mention your poor Aunt Grace. Your face is so peaceful and innocent, I'd hardly believe it now." Grace reached her fingers out to touch the soft cheek of the baby in her arms, unable to keep the smile from her face.

Joseph had been born breech which had been the reason Sylvia had struggled so much with the birth. It had been scary but, thankfully, both mother and baby had come through it. Grace knew how awful it had been but she also knew that Sylvia wouldn't have traded anything if it meant she'd been given this baby to love.

She knew soon the rest of the family would be swooping in to see the new baby so Grace was enjoying these few moments alone with her nephew. After her day, all she wanted was to hold on to this angel and forget about everything else.

Her confrontation with Connor this morning had weighed on her all day. She couldn't understand why he had decided to turn her life upside down when he'd made it clear he wasn't interested in anything more than friendship with her.

Yet, he offered to marry her to help her adopt the children. The moment she'd dreamed of for so long was nothing more than an offhanded proposal that meant nothing to him.

Her day had been ruined before it had barely began, then Henry had come at lunch to tell her he'd sent a wire to a judge in Oregon City and wasn't sure how things were going to turn out for the adoption.

Every time she looked at Oliver or Lizzie, her heart broke. She wanted to give these children the love they needed. And they had no idea how hard she was fighting for them. They still believed they were to be sent to an orphanage and it killed her not being able to give them the hope of something else.

But she was afraid to say anything to them and get their hopes up if they would just be crushed in the end.

"So, Connor stopped by earlier to see the baby."

Immediately, Grace's guard went up. She knew her brother was about to get at something she wasn't ready to talk about.

"That was nice of him."

She kept her eyes on Joseph, not wanting the spell to be broken that had woven around them while she held him.

They sat in silence for a while and she knew her brother wasn't going to let it go. He had something to say and she knew what he was like. She may as well just face him. She lifted her eyes and shrugged. "I know you've got something to say to me, so just go ahead."

"You make me sound like I'm some kind of old ogre who always bosses you around. Honestly, Grace, you know I've always only wanted the best for you. After Pa died, it was my responsibility to take care of things."

Grace swallowed, remembering back to when Luke had sent her west to protect her from their uncle who was abusive to her and Phoebe. He'd taken his job as older brother seriously and had done everything to give them a better life.

"Connor has told me about your decision to adopt the Harvey children. While I was a bit shocked to hear it, I've had some time to think. And, if it's what you want to do, you have my support. I will do whatever I can to help. I believe you could give those children a wonderful home."

Grace's mouth opened in surprise. She'd expected her brother to fight her decision at every turn, thinking her too young or unable to raise the children without a man to help her.

She looked suspiciously at Sylvia who sat beside Luke smiling at her. Grace had no doubt her friend had a hand in talking sense into her brother and she sent her a silent thank you.

"However, there is something else I need to talk about. And I know you're going to get a bit hot-headed about it, so I'm telling you now to just sit and listen without arguing."

Grace cringed, closing her eyes briefly. She should have known that was too easy.

"Connor said he asked you to marry him." Luke threw his hand up to stop her from interrupting. "He admitted he's made a lot of mistakes when it comes to you and he takes responsibility for the mess he says he made. But, he also told me some things today I think you need to hear."

"Luke, I know Connor is a friend of yours and you both spent a lot of time together down in California. I've known him a long time too, even though he left all those years ago. But I remember who he was before he went down there. And he's not the same man who returned."

Luke shook his head sadly. "No, Grace, he isn't."

"Well, I can't help what happened to him. He's the one that's been holding on to all that pain and letting it ruin his chance to ever move forward in life."

She was getting angry talking about it again. It seemed like that's all it ever was with Connor. How he'd suffered so much in that fire and now with the scars he carried.

"Grace, sometimes it's not just as easy as you

think. Yes, Connor is holding on to a lot of pain from what happened to him. But there was more than that. The thing is, he was engaged to be married when that fire happened. And after, she left him because she couldn't stand to look at him anymore."

Her heart pounded in her ears. She was sure everyone else in the room could hear it with the silence that now hung over them. Her stomach clenched in pain.

"He told you that?" Her words barely came out over the lump in her throat.

Luke nodded. "He said he'd never wanted to tell anyone about it because of the hurt and embarrassment. He knew people were already pitying him for what had happened and for what he now had to live with every day. He didn't want anyone to know he'd lost so much more that day. After that happened, he didn't think he was ever worthy of a woman. He'd thought she loved him but had been able to get rid of him so easily simply because she couldn't look at him."

The room around her seemed like it was closing in on her. "Why didn't he tell me? Surely he knew I would never be like that."

Luke laughed sharply. "Grace, when a man has

been hurt like that, he isn't likely to ever trust that someone else won't do the same to him. I'm sure he wanted to tell you but knew you'd just deny feeling like that. He said he never wanted you to end up having to regret being with him or someday looking at him the same way she had."

Grace couldn't believe what she was hearing. If he would have told her, she could have shown him she would never be like that other woman.

"Well, I will talk to him. I couldn't have known."

Luke shook his head. "That's the thing, Grace. I don't know if you'll be able to talk to him. He came here to say goodbye. He said he needed to go away for a while until he knew he was finally free of the past. He didn't want to hurt anyone anymore."

Her chest ached as she listened to her brother. She stood up and handed Joseph to Sylvia's waiting arms. "He's not getting off that easy. He can't always just run from his problems. Did he say where he was going?"

"No, but you're not going anywhere. It's winter and it's dark. What do you possibly think you can do?"

She wasn't listening as she opened the door.

Her brother wasn't going to tell her what she could or couldn't do. Not over something like this.

She wasn't letting Connor leave without at least trying to talk to him one more time.

CHAPTER 17

"Oh, Mrs. Larsen, I was hoping you could tell me where Connor is?" Grace stopped at the bottom of the stairs as the boardinghouse owner came down with her arms full of laundry.

"I'm afraid I can't, Grace. He came to me earlier and paid up his bill and said he was leaving for a while. I was just bringing the bedding down and was going to clean out his room."

Grace held onto the railing as she tried to think of what to do next. Just then, Henry walked around the corner toward the dining room. "Grace, what a surprise! Would you care to join me for a bite? I was going to come see you tomorrow to tell you the news but can let you know now since you're here."

"I'm sorry, but I don't have time to stop. What is the news?"

"I heard back from the judge and all we need to do is sign all the paperwork and the Harvey children will be in your care. It will take a bit longer to get the adoption papers filled out but he says there shouldn't be any problems, so for now, the children are yours. We can let them know tomorrow and, as long as everyone is willing, they can start coming to stay with you any time."

Grace brought her hand to her mouth to hold back the sob of happiness. "Thank you so much, Henry. I truly appreciate your help with everything."

"Well, does that mean you'll join me in a celebration?"

She wished she could but, right now, she had to find Connor. She was thrilled about finding out the children would be hers but they weren't the only ones she cared about. Connor had her heart and, if she didn't at least try to catch up to him somehow, she knew she would always regret it.

"Mrs. Larsen, did he leave anything in his room to indicate where he might be going?"

The other woman shook her head. "Not that I saw, but you're welcome to go up and look. I haven't cleaned anything up yet."

Grace looked at Henry as she moved onto the first step. "I will look forward to seeing you tomorrow. Perhaps we can wait until after school and go out to the farm then."

He nodded, obviously aware she wasn't going to join him to eat as she raced up the stairs.

"It's the second door on the left, Grace." Mrs. Larsen hollered up the stairs after her as she got to the top.

The door was still open so Grace stepped into the room, her heart clenching as she thought about the man who'd been staying here. What if she couldn't find him?

She started moving around the room, opening drawers and looking behind everything. There was nothing left that she could see. He'd packed everything up.

Moving to the chair by the window, she sat down, trying to calm her racing heart. She had no idea of where to even look for him. If he'd left hours ago, there wasn't much chance she was going to find him in the dark.

Her eyes landed on the trash can where, just on the outside, sat a crumpled-up piece of paper that had been thrown away. She reached down, hoping it might give her some kind of clue.

As she pressed it open, her heart stopped and

her breath caught in her throat. She realized what it was and, though she knew she shouldn't be reading it, her eyes were already moving along the paper.

My Dear Connor

I wish there was some other way I could say these words, however I know you would make it hard on me to do it in person. So, I'm writing them down to save myself the pain of having to face any kind of argument.

Since your accident, I've stood by you but the time has come for me to be honest. We are not suited to be married and I'm leaving on the stagecoach today to go stay at my grandmother's in New York.

Every time I see you, I see the disfigurement and while I never believed me to be a vain woman, I fear I can't see past it. When we are in public, people stare and I know what they're thinking. I hope in time your scars will fade, to make life a little easier for you but, right now, it's too much for me to bear.

While I'd always told myself I would be happy enough staying here and being married to a black-smith, the truth is, I long for a more exciting life in a city, with people who would enjoy the theater and other forms of entertainment. I believe the accident has helped to open my eyes to know what's in my heart.

I wish things could be different but I know I could never see past the outer scars. I can't stay with you out of pity because it wouldn't be fair to either of us.

I wish you all the best.

Sincerely,

Irene

Grace's hands shook as she held the paper. Anger, pain, hurt...every emotion Connor had to have felt as he'd read these words for the first time overcame her.

If this woman were standing in front of her right now, Grace knew she'd be doing something very unladylike to her.

She dropped her head into her hands, fighting back the tears for what he'd gone through. He'd lost someone dear to him in the fire and had to relive it over and over in his mind. He suffered the pain of his injuries and been left with scars to remind him every time he looked in the mirror. Then, the one person who should have loved him beyond all that hurt him even more.

And the part that caused her own heartache was knowing she'd never given him the chance to work through it all, pushing him away before he could have the time to believe she would be any different.

"I wanted to tell you about Irene but I was embarrassed."

Her head snapped up as Connor's voice reached her ears. She jumped to her feet and walked over to him, reaching out to take his hands.

"You're here! I thought you'd left."

He shrugged then smiled. "I did. But I came back because I forgot something."

She couldn't think of what he'd possibly forgotten because she'd searched every inch of this room but she didn't care. He was standing here now and she wasn't letting him go.

"I forgot to tell you how much I love you. I forgot to let you know that, even though my marriage proposal might have been made in haste and for different reasons than you believed, I promise you, I meant it. I wanted to marry you, not out of a sense of obligation. But because I love you. Because I know you're the only woman who has ever loved me for who I am, seeing beyond everything else. And, because I know you're the only woman I could ever love the way I do."

Her heart raced and the tears she'd held back slid down her cheeks. She sobbed as she tried to find her own words.

"I'm sorry for pushing you away. I love you too, Connor. I've loved you since I was thirteen years old and, even though I didn't think it was possible, I think I fall even more in love with you every time I see you. I wish you could have told me everything but I know how hard it must have been for you. I promise you, the love I feel for you will never be out of pity. When I look at you, I see the face of a man I know who is kind and who would take the time to make sure a school is warmed up every morning for the teacher and students. A man who would take the time to look in the bushes for a marble because it was important to someone. And, I see a man who went through pain but never let it change his heart."

He pulled his hands from hers, then reached around her waist to pull her to him. As his head lowered and his lips covered hers, Grace knew that the wait had been worth it.

She had the love of the only man who could ever have her heart. And she was never letting him go.

EPILOGUE

"It was so hard not to say anything to the children all day. They've been so sad, thinking they were going to still be going to the orphanage. I wanted to tell them so many times, just to see their happiness return."

Grace stopped talking, bringing her hand up to her chest as she slowly turned to look at Connor in the seat beside her. "They will be happy, won't they? I never really thought about how they might feel."

Connor reached over and took her hand, giving it a gentle squeeze before taking control of the reins again. "These children will be happier than they've likely been in a very long time to find out they will have you as their ma."

They were on their way out to the Harvey

farm to tell the children. She'd gone right after school to sign all the paperwork she had to for now, then told Henry that Connor would take her out to break the exciting news.

She wasn't entirely sure but she thought she might have seen a flicker of jealousy in the lawyer's eyes but it didn't matter to her at all. There was nothing any other man could offer her to take her away from this man beside her.

After he'd come back to the boardinghouse and they'd had a chance to work things out, they had gone over to Luke's to let him know what had happened.

Apparently, Connor had made it to the farm to talk with his ma and told her he would be leaving again for a while.

Anna Wallace had sat him down and given him a stern talking to and he said he'd felt like he was five years old again getting a scolding. She'd told him what a fool he was being and had informed him she had known from the day Grace had shown up in Bethany that she was the one for him.

It had just taken them a bit longer to figure it out.

He'd realized after speaking to his mother that he needed to at least tell Grace how he felt before he left, to see if there was any chance to make things right. So, he'd turned around and came back to town, going to her place, then Luke's, before finding her in his room at the boardinghouse.

Every time she replayed the moment he'd told her he loved her, her heart would swell with happiness. She couldn't believe how close she'd come to letting it get away from her.

But, she knew now she was never going to let that happen. No matter what arguments or worries that might try to come between them, she knew they could work them out.

The rundown farmhouse came into view and Grace quickly looked at Connor. "What if they're too upset about leaving their grandma? Or, what if they think I won't be able to look after them? I mean, I only have the one bedroom in my house but I am going to get a bed moved into the main room and the children can share the room. Luke said he'd help me..."

"Grace, stop. You're going to be fine. Trust me. Those children already love you. They will know they can still visit their grandmother all the time and that's the best gift you could give them. And for Mrs. Harvey, She will know her grandchildren will be well taken care of and she will still get to be in their lives. You're giving them a family and someone who will always love them. So, take a deep breath and enjoy this moment when you get to tell them they're coming to live with you."

They pulled to a stop and Grace took a moment to calm her nerves before Connor reached up to help her down. He placed his hands on her waist and lifted her down, holding her for a second as he smiled down at her. "If those children end up loving you even half as much as I do, they're going to be the happiest children in the world."

She couldn't help the smile that spread across her face. He stepped back and let her go to the door, holding his hand on her back. Mrs. Harvey opened it wide to let them in.

"Miss Hamilton! What are you doing out here?" Lizzie ran over to hug her legs. "Is Oliver in trouble for something?"

Oliver stood to the side, his eyes wide as he hoped what his sister was asking wasn't true.

Grace looked at Mrs. Harvey to see if it was all right to tell the children now. They'd both signed the papers today and she knew how happy the older woman was for how everything had worked out. Tears filled her eyes as she nodded at

Grace, so thankful to know her grandchildren would be loved and cared for.

Grace crouched down so she could be eye to eye with Lizzie. She motioned with her hand toward Oliver. "Come over here for a moment, Oliver. I'd like to talk to you and your sister."

The poor boy looked skeptical, still unsure why his teacher wanted to talk to him. She had to hold back the laughter as he searched his memory for something that might have caused him to possibly be in trouble.

But, he came over like she asked and stood beside his sister, pushing his hands into his pants pockets.

"Children, I wanted to talk to you about something and I hope you will be as happy as I am about it." She quickly glanced up and caught Connor's eye. He winked and gave her an encouraging smile. "I've been speaking with your grandma and we thought that maybe instead of going to live in an orphanage in Oregon City, you might be happier if you could stay here in Bethany. And live with me."

Both children stared at her, still confused about what she was saying. Lizzie pulled her eyebrows together. "But why would we live with you?"

Grace swallowed, hoping she could get this right. "Well, I want to give you both a home. I know I could never replace your real mother but, if you'll let me, I'd like to be your ma."

Lizzie looked at Oliver, waiting to see his reaction before she decided. Grace held her breath, hoping they would be happy with the news. She knew they'd likely spent the past few days coming to terms with the reality of having to go live in an orphanage, so they were likely feeling confused.

Oliver stepped over a bit closer and she could see wetness in his eyes. "Do you mean, you want us to live with you, forever? And we could stay here, in Bethany? And still see our Grandma?" His voice started to shake as he looked up at Mrs. Harvey who came over and put her arm around him.

"Yes, dear. Miss Hamilton is going to give you a home with her. And that means, we'll all still get to be together to visit and to still be family."

Oliver reached up to quickly wipe at his eyes, trying desperately not to let anyone see him cry. Connor walked over and put his hand on his shoulder as Mrs. Harvey moved over to stand beside Lizzie.

The little girl started to cry, then jumped into

Grace's arms, almost knocking her over backward. "Thank you, Miss Hamilton. I promise I'll be a good girl and I will help around the house."

Oliver was nodding. "And I'll help to do the things a man would do around the house too. We'll work hard, we promise."

Grace laughed, reaching out to pull Oliver over to her. "Children, you know what I'd like the most from you both?"

They shook their heads as they stood looking at her.

"I want you to be children. And to have fun, and play, and sometimes help me with chores around the house if I ask. But most of all, I just want you to be happy and to let me be the best ma I can. It's going to take me a while to learn how to be a ma because I've never done it before. So, maybe you can both teach me what I need to know."

Lizzie giggled, then hugged her again, pushing her face into Grace's shoulder. "I think you're going to be a great ma."

Oliver was still standing back, just in front of her. She could see the indecision in his eyes about whether or not he could hug her. Until now, she'd been his teacher. And, he was a boy so showing his emotions wasn't as easy for him.

She pulled him in closer, letting his skinny arms wrap around her neck too. Her heart had never felt as full as it did in this moment. When she looked up and saw Connor grinning down at her, she knew she truly had everything she could have ever wanted.

Some men might have run the other direction knowing the woman they'd just professed their love to was still going ahead and adopting two children.

But, Connor was here. And the joy on his face was for her, knowing how much this had meant to her.

Finally, the children stepped back and went to hug their grandma who had tears streaming down her face too. Connor put his hand out to help Grace back up to standing, then continued to hold it as they stood and watched the family together.

Lizzie came over again and reached up for Connor's other hand. He took it, smiling down at the little girl who was looking up at him seriously.

"So, does this mean you're going to be our pa?"

Grace's mouth dropped open in embarrassment but the child was asking an innocent question because she truly didn't know any better. She quickly turned to give Connor an apologetic smile.

He lifted his eyes and met hers, his face not showing any embarrassment at all. Finally, he nodded slowly, never taking his eyes from hers.

"Well, Lizzie, I sure do hope so. But, that's going to depend on your ma. Because the thing is, I really love her and there's nothing I'd love more than to marry her. And to be your pa." He looked back down at the little girl who was still holding onto his hand. "If you'll let me."

Lizzie was nodding her head wildly and when Grace turned to look at Oliver, he came over, nodding too. "Oh, please Miss Hamilton. Can he be our pa?"

Grace laughed, then met Connor's gaze. In his eyes, she could see his heart, laid out for her to have. He wanted to offer these children what he could give too and she knew he didn't have to do it.

But, she could also tell this wasn't the reason he was wanting to marry her.

Without saying a word, she could see the love he was offering her if she would take it.

Finally, she nodded her head, unable to hold her own tears back any longer. "I'd love for him to be your pa."

Connor's mouth spread into a wide grin and he lifted Lizzie into his arms, spinning her around as she screamed with joy. Mrs. Harvey clapped her hands together, then moved faster than Grace had ever seen as she went over to the stove.

"Well, I'd say we all need to sit down and have a nice cup of tea and a slice of pie to celebrate. Oliver, you and Lizzie come here and help me set the table."

Grace smiled to herself as the older woman understood the need for the couple to have a moment to themselves, taking the excited children over to get their celebration ready.

She turned to face Connor as he took her hands and held them down between them. "Are you sure, Grace?"

In all the time she'd known Connor Wallace, she'd never heard words so unsure, yet so filled with hope.

"Connor, how can you even ask me that? I've always been sure."

He swallowed, bringing one of her hands up to gently kiss the back as he held it tight. "Thank you, Grace Hamilton. For helping me to live again and for everything you've given me."

She unhooked her fingers from his and lifted her hand to trace the skin on his cheek. So many words she wanted to say but she couldn't seem to get them past the lump in her throat.

"I haven't given you anything other than my heart."

He placed his hand over hers, leaning his head into her hand. "And that's the greatest gift I could have ever been given."

The spell was broken as Lizzie ran over and pulled them apart. "Come on! I helped Grandma make this apple pie and it's really good. I'll show you how to make it sometime, Miss Hamilton."

Grace looked at Connor and they both started to laugh. He shrugged, as the girl started to pull him over to the table. "I guess we will have to get used to having interruptions with two children under foot."

"Are you sure you want to do this, Connor? I know it wasn't really what you had agreed to, so I'd understand."

He was shaking his head as he sat down at the table, Oliver and Lizzie both clamoring over each other to be the one to serve him.

"I wouldn't give this up for anything."

Grace looked around the table at the happy faces next to her and knew she had everything she could have ever dreamed of. And maybe even a little bit more.

✿

THREE YEARS LATER

Grace held her baby in her arms, rocking as she looked out the window at the newly fallen snow. It seemed so peaceful in comparison to what was taking place inside the house where she sat. Thankfully, Connor had been sure to build a house big enough to hold the whole family when they were together because Grace knew there weren't many places that could.

They'd been married shortly after telling the children they were adopting them and, in the spring, he'd purchased some land just on the outskirts of town. Along with the Wallace men and Luke, it hadn't taken long for their new house to be built. Which was good because she'd had their first baby not long after the last log was hammered into place.

Now, they had another and Grace worried they might have to keep adding on as their family grew. Lizzie and Oliver had settled in nicely, letting her give them the home they needed. They now called her ma and every time she heard the word, it filled her heart with joy.

And, they'd taken on their roles as big brother

and sister very seriously, so she knew all of her children would never long for the love of a family.

Her eyes moved around the large room where everyone had gathered after the baby's christening. Phoebe walked over and sat down beside her.

"It's hard to believe how much has happened since we got on with that wagon train all those years ago, isn't it? I can't even imagine our lives if we hadn't come here or ended up in Bethany. This little town on the other side of the country has become home to us."

Grace nodded, looking around at all the people who had become so dear to her. Not only the Wallace family but everyone else who was now a part of her life. Susan and James O'Hara, the kind older couple who had helped two young girls make it all the way to Oregon, then settled here too. Mrs. Harvey, who had become a part of the family. And all of the other townspeople who had made Bethany the home they'd always dreamed of.

She smiled at her sister, reaching out to take her hand. "Thank you for bringing me here. I think ma and pa would be happy to know how things turned out for all of us."

Luke came over and sat down beside them. "What are you girls talking about?"

KAY P. DAWSON

Grace laughed, shaking her head at her brother. "Oh, just about how mad we were at you when you made us go find some strange man to take us on a wagon train to Oregon. And how, if you hadn't been such a stubborn man and actually listened to our arguments, how different our lives would have been."

The three of them looked around at the chaos that was the Wallace family and smiled, knowing there was nowhere else they would rather be than under the blue Oregon skies.

IF YOU LIKED THIS, YOU MAY ENJOY: EVERLY

WILDER WEST BOOK ONE

A SWEET, CLEAN, MAIL-ORDER BRIDE ROMANCE!

The terms of her father's will leave Everly with no choice but to marry before her 21st birthday to ensure the security of her family.

Will she be able to get over her anger towards men in enough time to find someone to marry?

Answering an ad for a mail-order bride, she finds Ben – a man who needs a woman to help him raise his two nieces left in his care. Can they find love while dealing with both a vindictive step-mother who wants to stop her from marrying, and a meddling woman who is determined to take the children from Ben? They will both have to learn to trust, even as the past threatens to ruin everything.

"Tangles of emotions, a little bit of suspense and then a happy ending! Everything to make a beautiful clean romance set in the old west!" – **Reader**

AVAILABLE NOW!

ABOUT THE AUTHOR

USA Today Bestselling Author, Kay P. Dawson writes sweet western romance – the kind that leaves out all of the juicy details and immerses you in a true, heartfelt love story. Growing up pretending she was Laura Ingalls, she's always had a love for the old west and pioneer times. She believes in true love, and finding your happy ever after.

Happily married mom of two girls, Kay has always taught her children to follow their dreams. And, after a breast cancer diagnosis at the age of 39, she realized it was time to take her own advice. She had always wanted to write a book, and she decided that the someday she was waiting for was now.

She writes western historical, contemporary and time travel romance that all transport the reader to a time or place where true love always finds a way.

www.ingramcontent.com/pod-product-compliance
Lightning Source LLC
Chambersburg PA
CBHW011451170626
46816CB00009B/2620